Contents

Max the Hairy Hero: A Journey of Courage and Destiny

Once upon a time, in a small village nestled in the heart of a dense forest, there lived a young boy named Max. Max was unlike any other boy in the village. He was born with a dense layer of hair all over his body, which made him look more like a wild animal than a human being. The villagers feared him and often teased him for his appearance.

Max sighed, "Why does everyone in this village hate me? What have I done to deserve this?"

Max's mother comforted him, "Don't worry, Max. They are just scared of what they don't understand. You are a special boy, and you will find your place in this world someday."

Max felt a hope, "Really, Mama? Do you truly believe that?"

Max's mother smiles, "Yes, Max. I do. And I know that there is someone out there who will accept you just the way you are."

One day, while Max was out exploring the forest, he stumbled upon an old wizard who was in trouble. The wizard was being attacked by a group of vicious wolves. Max, being a brave and kind-hearted boy, rushed to the wizard's aid and fought off the wolves.

Wizard said gratefully "Thank you, young man. You have saved my life."

Max smiled, "It was nothing, sir. I couldn't just stand by and watch you get hurt."

Wizard was impressed, "You have a kind heart and a brave spirit, Max. I can sense great things in your future."

Max surprised, "Really, sir?"

Wizard nodded, "Yes, Max. You are not just any ordinary boy. You are a special boy with unique abilities. And I have a feeling that you will be called upon to use those abilities to save this kingdom from great peril."

Max excited, "What do you mean, sir? What abilities do I have?"

Wizard smiled mysteriously, "All will be revealed in due time, Max. For now, just know that you have a great destiny ahead of you. And I will be here to guide you every step of the way."

Max felt a new sense of hope and excitement for the future. He knew that he was not just a hairy boy, but a special boy with a great destiny. And he was determined to find out what that destiny was and fulfill it with all his might.

As Max grew older, he learned more about his abilities and how to control them. The wizard had trained him in the ways of magic and combat, and Max had become a skilled warrior.

One day, a dark sorcerer named Zoltar emerged and threatened to take over the kingdom. Zoltar had an army of dark creatures and was determined to conquer all the lands. The villagers were scared and didn't know what to do.

Max stepped forward, "I will stop Zoltar and save our kingdom."

A villager was skeptical, "How can you possibly stop him, Max? He's too powerful."

Ma was confident, "I have the wizard's training and my own abilities. I will not let our kingdom fall."

The wizard appeared beside Max and nodded in agreement.

Wizard said with encouraging voice, "Max is the only one who can stop Zoltar. He is the only one who has the strength and the courage to defeat him."

Max set off on his quest to stop Zoltar and save the kingdom. He faced many challenges along the way, but he never lost sight of his goal. Finally, he arrived at Zoltar's castle and prepared for the ultimate battle.

Zoltar laughed, "So, the hairy boy thinks he can defeat me? How quaint."

Max determined, "I may be just a hairy boy, but I have the courage and strength to defeat you and save my kingdom."

And with that, the battle began. Max used all his training and abilities to fight against Zoltar and his dark creatures. It was a fierce battle, but Max never lost hope. In the end, Max emerged victorious and Zoltar was defeated.

Max said, "The kingdom is safe now."

A villager was grateful, "Thank you, Max. You truly are a hero."

Max returned to the village as a hero, and the villagers celebrated his victory. From that day on, Max was no longer just a hairy boy. He was a hero, a protector of the kingdom, and a symbol of hope for all.

With Zoltar defeated, the kingdom was once again at peace. Max was hailed as a hero and was celebrated throughout the land. The villagers no longer feared him, but instead admired and respected him for his bravery and strength.

Max continued to live in the village, but he also traveled to other lands, helping those in need and fighting against evil wherever he found it. He became known as the "Hairy Hero" and his legend spread far and wide.

One day, the wizard approached Max and said:

Wizard smiled, "Max, it is time for you to take your place as the leader of this kingdom. You have proven yourself to be a wise and just ruler, and the people trust and respect you."

Max surprised, "Me, a ruler? Are you sure, sir?"

Wizard nodded, "Yes, Max. You have the strength and the wisdom to lead this kingdom to greatness. And I have no doubt that you will do so with honor and justice."

And so, Max became the ruler of the kingdom and led it to a time of prosperity and peace. He ruled with fairness and kindness, and his people loved him for it.

Max reflected himself, "I never thought that I, a hairy boy, would become a hero and a ruler. But I am grateful for my journey and for the destiny that was given to me."

Max lived the rest of his life as a beloved ruler and a revered hero. And his legend lived on, inspiring future generations to be brave and to follow their own destinies, no matter what obstacles they may face.

The End.

The Songbird Princess

Once upon a time, there was a young princess named Amara who lived in a kingdom far, far away. Amara was special because she loved to sing, and her voice was so beautiful that everyone who heard it was filled with joy and wonder.

One day, the king and queen of the kingdom announced that they were looking for a prince who would marry their daughter and become the future king. But Amara was not interested in finding a husband. All she wanted to do was sing.

Amara: "Father, Mother, I do not want to marry. I want to sing and share my gift with the world."

King: "But my dear, you must marry. It is the tradition of our kingdom and it is your duty as a princess."

Queen: "Yes, and besides, you will have many opportunities to sing for your husband and the people of the kingdom."

Amara: "But what if I marry someone who does not appreciate my singing? I cannot bear the thought of giving up my passion."

The king and queen were saddened by their daughter's refusal to follow tradition, but they loved her and wanted her to be happy. So, they came up with a solution. They would hold a singing competition and whoever impressed Amara the most with their love for music would become her prince.

King: "Very well, my daughter. We will hold a singing competition. The one who impresses you the most with their love for music will become your prince."

Queen: "And the winner will not only win your hand in marriage, but they will also become the future king of our kingdom."

Amara was overjoyed. Finally, she would have the chance to marry someone who truly appreciated her love for music. The kingdom was buzzing with excitement as princes from far and wide came to compete for the hand of the Songbird Princess. And so, the search for the prince who loved music as much as Amara began.

The competition was fierce, with princes from all over the kingdom showing off their musical skills. But none of them were able to win Amara's heart with their singing. They were all too focused on impressing her and becoming the future king, but they forgot about the most important thing: Amara's love for music.

Amara: "None of them understand my passion for singing. They are all trying to win my hand, but they do not understand what music means to me."

Queen: "Do not worry, my daughter. The right prince will come along. You will know it when you hear his voice."

And then, on the final day of the competition, a young prince named Lucas stepped forward to sing. As he began to sing, Amara was amazed. His voice was like nothing she had ever heard before. He sang with all his heart, and it was clear that he truly loved music.

Amara: "That's it! That's the voice I've been looking for! He sings from his heart, he loves music as much as I do!"

King: "Lucas, is it true that you love music as much as my daughter?"

Lucas: "Yes, Your Majesty. I have been singing since I was a child, and music is my life. I have never met someone who loves music as much as I do, until I met Princess Amara. I will cherish her love for music and support her in all her musical endeavors."

Amara and Lucas locked eyes, and they both knew that they had found the one they had been searching for. The king and queen were overjoyed, and they immediately declared Lucas the winner of the competition.

Amara and Lucas were married in a grand ceremony, and the entire kingdom was filled with music and joy. The people of the kingdom loved their new prince and princess, and they sang and danced together in celebration.

Years passed, and Amara and Lucas ruled the kingdom with love and fairness. They continued to sing together and share their love for music with the people of the kingdom. They inspired others to pursue their passions and to never give up on their dreams.

Queen: "My dear daughter, you have found happiness and fulfilled your passion for music. I am so proud of you."

King: "And Lucas, you have proven to be a true prince, and a loving husband to our daughter. You have our blessings and our support."

Lucas: "Thank you, Your Majesties. I am grateful for your daughter and for the love and support of this kingdom."

Amara: "I am the luckiest princess in all the land. I have found my prince, and we have found each other's passion for music. Together, we will make beautiful music for the rest of our lives."

And so, Amara and Lucas lived happily ever after, sharing their love for music with the kingdom and inspiring others to follow their dreams.

The end.

The Stone and the Wolf's Wager

Once upon a time, in a vast and dense forest, there lived a sly and cunning wolf. He was known to be the fastest and most agile animal in the forest, and he often boasted about his swiftness and agility to other animals.

One day, while the wolf was out for a hunt, he came across a big and heavy stone lying beside a river. The wolf sneered at the stone and said, "Ha! You are nothing but a useless rock. You can't even move an inch on your own. I bet I could run circles around you in no time!"

The stone, being a proud and haughty entity, took offense to the wolf's words and retorted, "I may not be able to run, but I bet I can stay in one place longer than you can run without stopping. And if you lose, you will have to admit that I am the superior one."

The wolf, always eager for a challenge, accepted the bet without hesitation. And so, the two began their wager, with the wolf running as fast as he could and the stone steadfastly staying in its place.

For what felt like hours, the wolf ran and ran, his endurance and speed never waning. However, just when he thought he had won the bet, he stumbled and fell, exhausted and out of breath. The stone, meanwhile, had remained in its place, unmoved and unshaken.

The wolf, defeated, lay on the ground panting, and the stone spoke with a proud and triumphant voice, "Ha! I have won the bet. You may be fast and agile, but you cannot beat the power of perseverance and determination. I am the true winner here."

And so, the wolf learned a valuable lesson that day, and from then on, he never again underestimated the strength of a seemingly immovable object.

The wolf, being a proud and determined animal, was not willing to admit defeat so easily. He had to find a way to prove himself superior to the stone once and for all. So, he came up with a plan to trick the stone into moving from its place.

Wolf: "Stone, I have a proposition for you. I challenge you to a race, but this time, the winner will be determined by the distance we cover, not the time we stay still."

Stone: "Ha! That's an easy challenge for me. I may not be able to move, but I can be carried. So, I accept your challenge."

The race began, with the wolf carrying the stone on his back, determined to cover as much distance as he could. But as they ran, the wolf realized that the stone was much heavier than he had anticipated. He began to tire, and his pace slowed down. Just then, the stone spoke up.

Stone: "Wolf, I have a confession to make. I may not be as strong as you, but I am much smarter. I have been using my weight to slow you down and tire you out. And now, I have won the race."

Wolf: "What?! That's not fair! You tricked me!"

Stone: "Ha! The true measure of a winner is not just physical strength but also wit and cunning. And in that, I have proven myself to be the superior one."

The wolf, defeated and humbled, admitted defeat and praised the stone for its cunning and intelligence. From that day on, the wolf and the stone became fast friends, and the wolf never again underestimated the power of perseverance and determination.

And so, the story of the stone and the wolf's wager came to an end, but it served as a reminder that sometimes, the true measure of strength lies not in physical ability but in wit and determination.

After the race, the wolf and the stone spent the rest of the day together, talking and laughing. The wolf was impressed by the stone's wit and intelligence, and the stone was impressed by the wolf's physical strength and agility.

Wolf: "I never would have thought that a stone could be so clever and cunning. I have truly learned a valuable lesson today."

Stone: "And I never would have thought that a wolf could be so humble and quick to admit defeat. It takes true strength to acknowledge one's weaknesses and learn from them."

From that day on, the wolf and the stone became fast friends, and they spent many days exploring the forest and having adventures together. They learned to appreciate each other's strengths and to value the importance of determination and perseverance.

And whenever they encountered other animals who underestimated the power of determination and perseverance, the wolf and the stone would tell their story and share the lessons they had learned. The other animals would listen, wide-eyed and inspired, and they too would learn to value the strength of the mind and the heart over physical ability.

And so, the story of the stone and the wolf's wager became a beloved tale, passed down from generation to generation, serving as a reminder that sometimes, the greatest strength lies in the determination and perseverance of the heart.

The end.

The Magic Cup of the Three Princesses

Once upon a time, there was a kingdom ruled by a kind and just king. The king had three daughters, each more beautiful and kind-hearted than the last. Despite their beauty and goodness, the three princesses felt as if something was missing from their lives.

One day, an old wise woman approached the princesses and told them of a magical cup that would grant their deepest desires. The cup was located in a far-off kingdom, guarded by a fierce dragon.

The princesses were determined to find the cup, and so they set out on a journey to retrieve it. Along the way, they encountered many challenges and obstacles, but with their wit and bravery, they were able to overcome them all.

Finally, they arrived at the kingdom where the cup was kept. The dragon guarding the cup was massive and terrifying, but the princesses did not give up. They approached the dragon and spoke to it with kindness and respect, asking it to let them retrieve the cup.

To their surprise, the dragon listened to them and allowed them to take the cup, telling them that it was the goodness in their hearts that had convinced it to trust them.

The three princesses were overjoyed and thanked the dragon for its kindness. They returned to their kingdom and used the magic cup to make their deepest desires come true. From that day forward, they lived happily ever after, bringing joy and happiness to all those around them.

The three princesses soon discovered that the magic cup had a strange power. Whenever they used it, the cup would grant their wish, but at a great cost. The kingdom began to suffer as crops failed, the rivers ran dry, and the people became ill.

The three princesses realized that they had made a terrible mistake and that their actions had brought harm to their kingdom. They gathered together to find a solution and decided to seek the advice of the wise woman who had told them of the magic cup.

Wise Woman: "My dearest princesses, I am afraid the magic cup has a terrible curse. It only grants wishes at a great cost, taking from others what it gives to you. The only way to break the curse is to return the cup to its rightful place and to undo all the harm that has been done."

First Princess: "But how can we undo the harm? We have caused so much suffering."

Wise Woman: "You must go on a journey of redemption, making amends with all those you have wronged and righting the wrongs you have committed. Only then will the curse be lifted."

The three princesses were determined to break the curse and set out on their journey of redemption. They traveled far and wide, helping those they had harmed and making amends for their mistakes.

As the three princesses continued on their journey, they were met with resistance and mistrust from some of the people they had wronged. However, the princesses persevered, showing kindness and compassion and earning back the trust of those they had harmed.

After a long and arduous journey, the three princesses finally returned to the kingdom where the magic cup was kept. They approached the dragon once again and told it of their journey and their desire to break the curse.

Dragon: "You have proven yourselves to be truly kind and deserving of the magic cup's power. The curse is lifted, and the kingdom will flourish once again."

The dragon returned the magic cup to the princesses, and they used its power wisely and responsibly, bringing peace and prosperity to their kingdom. The people of the kingdom were grateful to the three princesses for their bravery and kindness, and they all lived happily ever after.

The end.

The Guardian and the Magic Spoon

Once upon a time, there was a young boy named Jon who lived in a small village with his parents. One day, while playing in the woods, Jon stumbled upon a strange object that looked like a spoon. He picked it up and took it home to show his parents.

"What is this, Mother?" asked Jon.

"It's just a spoon, dear," replied his mother.

But as Jon was about to put the spoon away, it suddenly started to glow. He was so amazed that he dropped the spoon, which then transformed into a beautiful golden rod with precious gems at one end.

"Mother, Father, come quick! Look what happened to the spoon," cried Jon.

His parents were just as surprised as he was, and they all wondered what the rod could be used for.

Just then, an old man appeared in their home. "That rod is a magic spoon," he said. "It will give you the power to do anything you wish, but be careful how you use it, for it can also bring great harm."

"What should we do with it?" asked Jon's father.

"Use it wisely and only for good, and you will have great wealth and happiness," said the old man. "But if you use it for evil, it will bring only misery and heartache."

With that, the old man disappeared. Jon and his parents were left with the magic spoon, and they knew that they had to be careful how they used it.

As Jon and his family began to use the magic spoon, news of their good deeds and wealth quickly spread throughout the land. Soon, they were sought after by many who wanted to use the spoon for their own selfish purposes.

One day, a wicked sorceress came to their village, seeking the magic spoon for her own evil plans. She threatened Jon and his family and told them that she would use the spoon to rule the kingdom with an iron fist if they did not hand it over.

But Jon was determined to protect the spoon from falling into the wrong hands, and so he set out on a quest to find a place where it would be safe from the sorceress. He encountered many obstacles along the way, including fierce beasts, treacherous mountains, and dark forests.

Finally, after many long months of traveling, Jon reached a hidden valley where he thought the magic spoon would be safe.

But as he was about to place the spoon in its hiding place, he was ambushed by the sorceress and her minions.

The sorceress tried to take the magic spoon by force, but Jon was not willing to give up so easily. He used the power of the spoon to defeat the sorceress and her minions in a great battle. In the end, Jon emerged victorious, and the sorceress was defeated, and the magic spoon was safely hidden away for all time.

With the sorceress defeated and the kingdom safe, Jon and his family began to relax and enjoy their newfound fame and wealth. But they soon realized that the battle against evil was far from over. There were still many people in the kingdom who sought to use the spoon for their own selfish purposes, and Jon knew that he must be ever vigilant in order to protect it.

So, Jon and his family continued to use the magic spoon for good, always on the lookout for those who sought to use it for evil. They became known as the guardians of the spoon, and their reputation as heroes spread far and wide. And they lived happily ever after, always using the power of the magic spoon to bring happiness and prosperity to the kingdom.

The end.

The Adventures of Tim and Tom

Once upon a time, in a kingdom far, far away, there lived two best friends named Tim and Tom. Tim was a kind-hearted soul who always looked for the good in others, while Tom was a mischievous and adventurous spirit who loved to explore the world.

One day, as Tim and Tom were playing in the forest, they stumbled upon a mysterious map. Excited at the prospect of adventure, they decided to follow the map in search of a hidden treasure.

As they journeyed through the forest, they encountered many challenges, including fierce beasts, treacherous rivers, and treacherous terrain. But through it all, they remained friends, always looking out for one another and encouraging each other when the going got tough.

Just when they thought they had reached the end of the trail, they came upon a large, imposing door that appeared to be the entrance to the treasure. Tim and Tom looked at each other, their eyes shining with excitement and wonder. They knew that whatever lay behind that door, their friendship would see them through.

"Are you ready, Tom?" asked Tim.

"I was born ready, Tim," replied Tom with a grin.

And with that, they opened the door, eager to see what adventures lay ahead.

As Tim and Tom continued their quest for the hidden treasure, they encountered even greater challenges and obstacles. They had to outwit dangerous beasts, solve puzzles, and brave treacherous terrains.

But despite all of the obstacles they faced, their friendship only grew stronger. They encouraged each other and worked together to overcome every challenge that came their way.

One day, they came to a dark and gloomy cave, deep within the forest. The air was thick with a foreboding sense of danger, but Tim and Tom were undaunted.

"We're so close, Tim," said Tom. "I can feel it. The treasure must be just beyond this cave."

"We'll get through this together, Tom," replied Tim. "Like we always do."

As they made their way deeper into the cave, they suddenly heard a loud growl. A fierce dragon appeared before them, its eyes glowing with an evil light.

"So, you've come to steal my treasure, have you?" growled the dragon.

Tim and Tom looked at each other, and then back at the dragon.

"We're not here to steal anything," said Tim. "We're just on a quest for adventure and discovery."

"Ha!" laughed the dragon. "Well, I have a quest for you as well. If you can answer my riddle, I'll give you the treasure. But if you can't, you'll become my next meal."

With that, the dragon posed a riddle so difficult that even the smartest of scholars would have struggled to solve it. "I am light as a feather, yet the strongest man cannot hold me for much longer than a minute. What am I?"

But Tim and Tom were not just any adventurers. They were friends, and together, they worked to solve the riddle. And in the end, they succeeded.

"Breath."

The dragon was so impressed with their friendship and their cleverness that he decided to give them the treasure after all.

After solving the riddle and acquiring the treasure, Tim and Tom continued on their journey. They returned to the kingdom, where they were greeted as heroes. People from all over the land came to see the young adventurers and hear of their incredible journey.

With the treasure and their newfound fame, Tim and Tom could have easily gone their separate ways. But their friendship was too strong for that. Instead, they decided to use their newfound wealth to help others. They built schools and hospitals and helped the less fortunate in the kingdom.

And so, Tim and Tom became known not just for their bravery and their quest for adventure, but for their kindness and their generosity. They remained the best of friends, always there for each other, no matter what life brought their way.

The end.

The Winged Adventurer

Once upon a time, there was a young girl named Kathy who lived in a small village surrounded by lush green forests and rolling hills. Kathy was adventurous and curious, always eager to explore and discover new things.

But what set Kathy apart from others was her love for flying. She would spend hours gazing at the sky, dreaming of soaring through the clouds and experiencing the freedom of flight.

Kathy: "Mother, have you ever seen a bird flying? It looks so free, soaring through the clouds, experiencing the wind in its feathers."

Mother: "Yes, my child. Flying is a wonderful experience. But it is not for humans."

Kathy: "But what if it could be, Mother? What if we could fly too?"

Mother: "My dear, humans do not have wings. We cannot fly like birds."

Kathy was determined to prove her mother wrong. She spent every moment she could studying birds and their flying patterns, hoping to learn their secrets.

One day, while exploring the forests, Kathy stumbled upon a magical tree. The tree was covered in shimmering leaves, and it pulsed with a soft, warm light. Kathy felt drawn to the tree, and as she approached, a voice spoke to her.

Voice: "Kathy, I have been waiting for you. I am the Tree of Flight, and I have the power to grant you the gift of flight."

Kathy was stunned. She had heard stories of the Tree of Flight, but she never thought she would find it.

Tree of Flight: "Do you wish to receive the gift of flight, Kathy?"

Kathy: "Yes, I do. More than anything in the world. I want to soar through the skies and experience the freedom of flight."

Tree of Flight: "Then come, place your hand on my trunk, and receive the gift of flight."

Kathy approached the tree and placed her hand on its trunk. She closed her eyes, and suddenly she felt a warm, comforting energy flow through her body. When she opened her eyes, she saw that she now had beautiful, shimmering wings.

Kathy: "I can fly! I can actually fly!"

And with that, Kathy spread her wings and took to the skies, soaring over the forests and hills, experiencing the freedom of flight for the first time. She had become the Winged Adventurer, and her journey was just beginning.

Kathy quickly became known as the Winged Adventurer, traveling from kingdom to kingdom, performing incredible flying feats and inspiring others to follow their dreams. However, she soon discovered that not everyone was happy with her newfound powers.

A wicked sorceress, known as Ravenna, had also heard of the Tree of Flight and the powers it granted. She was jealous of Kathy's abilities and determined to steal them for herself. Ravenna began to spread rumors and lies about Kathy, claiming that she was using her powers for evil.

One day, while flying over a kingdom, Kathy was suddenly attacked by a group of Ravenna's minions. She fought bravely, but they were too many, and she was forced to flee.

Kathy: "What is happening? Why is everyone turning against me?"

She flew as fast as she could, but the minions were hot on her trail. Just when she thought she couldn't escape, she was saved by a group of friendly fairies who offered to help her.

Fairy: "Do not worry, Winged Adventurer. We know the truth about Ravenna and her lies. We will help you defeat her and restore your good name."

Kathy was grateful for their help, and together they set out to stop Ravenna and clear her name.

Kathy and the fairies finally reached Ravenna's castle, where she was holding a grand ball in her honor. Kathy disguised herself as a servant and snuck into the castle to confront Ravenna.

Ravenna: "Ah, welcome my dear guests. Today we celebrate my victory over the Winged Adventurer. Soon, her powers will be mine, and no one will be able to stop me."

Kathy stepped forward, revealing her disguise.

Kathy: "Not so fast, Ravenna. I am the Winged Adventurer, and I have come to stop you and your evil plans."

Ravenna was furious and summoned her minions to attack Kathy. But with the help of the fairies, Kathy was able to defeat them and confront Ravenna in a magical battle.

The two clashed, their magic powers colliding in a dazzling display of light and color. In the end, Kathy emerged victorious, banishing Ravenna and restoring her good name.

Kathy: "It's over, Ravenna. Your reign of terror is over, and the truth about my powers has been revealed."

After defeating Ravenna, Kathy returned to her village as a hero. People from all over the kingdom came to celebrate her victory and thank her for restoring peace.

Kathy: "I never could have done it without the help of my friends and the support of all of you. Thank you for believing in me."

The villagers held a grand feast in Kathy's honor, and she was greeted with cheers and applause wherever she went.

In the following days, Kathy decided to use her powers for good and help others who, like her, had big dreams but didn't know how to make them come true. She became a mentor and guide, inspiring young girls to follow their hearts and pursue their passions, no matter how impossible they may seem.

Years passed, and Kathy's legend lived on, inspiring generations of young girls to chase their dreams and become the best versions of themselves. And the Winged Adventurer, who once only dreamed of flying, became a symbol of hope, courage, and determination.

Kathy: "I may have started this journey as the Winged Adventurer, but I am ending it as a role model for all young girls. And that, to me, is the greatest adventure of all."

The end.

The Boy Who Loved the Night

Once upon a time, in a kingdom where everyone loved the day and feared the night, there lived a young boy named Mason. Unlike everyone else, Mason was fascinated by the night. He loved the way the stars shone bright against the dark sky, and the peace and quiet that descended upon the kingdom after the sun went down.

Mason was often teased by the other children for his love of the night, but he didn't let it get him down. Instead, he continued to explore the kingdom at night, always seeking out new sights and sounds to experience.

One night, as Mason was wandering through the forest, he heard a strange noise. It was a voice, singing a haunting melody that filled Mason with both fear and wonder.

Curious, Mason followed the sound until he came upon a clearing in the forest. There, he saw a beautiful fairy, her wings shining like diamonds in the moonlight.

"Who are you?" asked Mason, his voice filled with wonder.

"I am the Guardian of the Night," replied the fairy. "And you, young boy, are the only one who has ever ventured into my domain. Why do you love the night so much?"

"It's just so peaceful and quiet," replied Mason. "And the stars are so beautiful."

The Guardian of the Night smiled at Mason. "I have a special gift for you," she said. "A gift that will allow you to see the night like never before."

And with that, the Guardian of the Night gave Mason a magic amulet that allowed him to see the night in all its glory. Mason was overjoyed, and he thanked the Guardian of the Night for her kindness.

From that night on, Mason explored the kingdom at night even more, always filled with wonder and excitement at all the amazing things he saw. And even though the other children still teased him, Mason didn't mind. He was too busy discovering the beauty of the night.

Mason soon discovered that the amulet not only allowed him to see the beauty of the night, but it also granted him special powers. He could communicate with the animals of the night, and they would come to him for help and advice.

Mason became known as the protector of the night creatures, and he was loved and respected by all. However, not everyone was happy with Mason's newfound powers. The king of the kingdom was jealous of Mason's popularity and the fact that Mason was the only one who could see the true beauty of the night.

The king ordered his army to capture Mason and bring him to the castle. Mason was thrown into a dark cell, and the amulet was taken from him.

Mason was determined to get the amulet back, so he used his powers to communicate with the night creatures. They came to his aid, and together, they fought their way through the castle to retrieve the amulet.

In the final battle, Mason stood face-to-face with the king. The king was wielding a sword, and Mason was armed only with his amulet.

"You can't defeat me, boy," sneered the king. "I am the ruler of this kingdom, and I will not be bested by a child."

"Maybe not," replied Mason, his voice filled with determination. "But I have something you don't have - the love and respect of the night creatures."

With that, Mason raised his amulet, and the night creatures descended upon the king, overwhelming him with their combined strength. The king was defeated, and Mason retrieved his amulet.

As Mason left the castle, the night creatures cheered and celebrated. Mason had proved himself to be a true hero, and the kingdom was safe once again.

With the king defeated, Mason was hailed as a hero throughout the kingdom. People came from far and wide to see him and thank him for his bravery.

Mason realized that he didn't need the amulet to see the beauty of the night. He had learned to appreciate it with his own eyes, and he felt grateful for the experience.

Mason decided to return the amulet to the Guardian of the Night. When he arrived in the forest, she greeted him with a smile.

"You have proven yourself to be a true friend of the night," she said. "And for that, I am proud of you."

Mason handed the amulet to the Guardian of the Night and thanked her for everything she had done for him.

"Keep exploring the night," she said with a smile. "And always remember the magic that lies within."

Mason left the forest, filled with a sense of peace and contentment. He had learned that true friendship and bravery came from within, and that the beauty of the night was something that could never be taken away.

And so, Mason lived the rest of his days exploring the kingdom at night, always in awe of the wonders that surrounded him. The kingdom never forgot the boy who loved the night, and he was remembered as a true hero for generations to come.

The end.

The Friendship of the Four Flowers

Once upon a time, in a land filled with vibrant flowers, there were four flowers who lived together in a beautiful garden. There was a rose, a lily, a daisy, and a sunflower. Despite their differences, the four flowers had become the best of friends and spent their days basking in the sun and enjoying each other's company.

One day, a terrible storm swept through the land, destroying everything in its path, including the garden where the four flowers lived. The flowers were separated and blown far apart from one another.

Rose: "Oh, how I miss my friends. I wonder where they are now."

Lily: "I am so lonely without my friends by my side. I hope they are safe."

Daisy: "I fear we may never see each other again."

Sunflower: "We must not give up hope. We must find each other and be together once again."

And so, the four flowers set out on a journey to find one another and be reunited as friends once again. They faced many challenges and obstacles along the way, but their determination and the memories of their friendship kept them going.

As the four flowers journeyed through the land, they encountered many other flowers and plants. Some were friendly and offered to help, while others were unkind and refused to assist. Despite the difficulties, the four friends never lost hope and continued their quest to be reunited.

Finally, after a long and arduous journey, the four flowers came across a beautiful meadow filled with the most vibrant and colorful flowers they had ever seen. In the center of the meadow stood a majestic tree, its branches reaching towards the sky.

Sunflower: "Look, my friends! The tree in the center of the meadow. It must hold the answer to our quest."

Lily: "Let us go and speak with the tree. Perhaps it can help us find one another."

The four flowers approached the tree and told it of their journey and their desire to be reunited with one another.

Tree: "I am the Guardian of the Garden, and I can help you. But first, you must each prove your friendship and show that it is strong enough to withstand any challenge."

The four flowers embarked on a series of trials and tests, each designed to test the strength of their friendship. They faced challenges and obstacles together, relying on one another for support and encouragement. Through their trials, the four flowers grew closer and their friendship grew stronger.

Finally, after all the trials had been completed, the tree declared the four flowers to be true friends and the guardians of the garden. It granted them the power to bring the garden back to life and restore the beauty that had been lost.

Tree: "The garden is yours to care for and protect. May your friendship continue to flourish and bring happiness to all who enter."

And so, the four friends worked together to bring the garden back to life. The flowers bloomed once again, and the garden became a place of beauty and peace. The four flowers continued to be the best of friends, always supporting and encouraging each other. They lived happily ever after, surrounded by the beauty of the garden they had brought back to life.

The end.

The Boy and the Goblins

Once upon a time, there was a boy named Andy who lived in a small village at the edge of a great forest. Andy was a curious boy who loved to explore the forest, and he often found himself in dangerous situations.

One day, Andy stumbled upon a group of goblins who were causing trouble in the forest. The goblins were known for their mischievous ways, and they had a reputation for being dangerous.

Andy was fascinated by the goblins, and he decided to approach them.

"Hello there!" said Andy, trying to be friendly.

The goblins sneered at him, showing their sharp teeth. "What do you want, boy?" one of them growled.

"I was just curious about you," replied Andy. "I've never seen goblins before."

The goblins laughed, and one of them stepped forward. "Well, now you have," he said. "And you won't be seeing us again, either."

With that, the goblins disappeared into the forest, leaving Andy alone. Andy was disappointed that the goblins had been so rude, but he was determined to learn more about them. He decided to set out on a journey to find them and try to make friends with them.

Andy traveled deep into the forest, following the trail of the goblins. He encountered many obstacles along the way, but he was determined to find the goblins and make friends with them.

As Andy journeyed deeper into the forest, he started to hear strange noises. It sounded like the goblins were in trouble. Andy picked up his pace, determined to help.

As Andy approached the source of the noise, he saw a group of goblins surrounded by a pack of wolves. The wolves were closing in on the goblins, and they were about to attack.

Andy sprang into action, using his wits and bravery to save the goblins from the wolves. The goblins were shocked by Andy's bravery, and they were amazed by his kindness.

"Who are you?" one of the goblins asked.

"I'm Andy," replied Andy, smiling. "I came to find you and make friends."

The goblins were taken aback by Andy's words, and they didn't know what to say. They had never met anyone like Andy before, and they were unsure of how to react.

The goblins were grateful to Andy for saving their lives, and they welcomed him into their group. They showed him their secret hideout in the forest, and they shared their stories and adventures with him.

Andy spent many days with the goblins, learning about their ways and enjoying their company. He was happy to have made new friends, and he was grateful for the experience.

One day, Andy realized that it was time for him to return home. The goblins were sad to see him go, but they understood.

"You're always welcome here," one of the goblins said. "And we'll always remember you as our friend."

Andy said goodbye to the goblins and set out for home. He was filled with a sense of peace and contentment, knowing that he had made new friends and learned new things.

And so, Andy lived the rest of his days exploring the forest and spreading the message of friendship. He was remembered by the goblins as a true hero, and he was loved by all who knew him.

The end.

The Magic Lake

Once upon a time, in a far-off kingdom, there was a boy named Sam who lived in a small village on the edge of a vast forest. Sam was a curious boy who loved to explore the forest and discover its secrets.

One day, while exploring the forest, Sam stumbled upon a small lake that was surrounded by ancient trees. The lake was calm and still, and it glimmered in the sunlight like a mirror. Sam was drawn to the lake, and he approached it with wonder and awe.

As Sam reached the edge of the lake, he noticed that the water was moving, as if there was something alive beneath its surface. Sam leaned forward to get a closer look, and he saw a figure rise from the water.

"Who are you?" asked Tom, taken aback by the sight.

The figure smiled at him, and its eyes twinkled. "I am the spirit of the lake," it said in a musical voice. "And I have been waiting for someone like you to come along."

Sam was fascinated by the spirit, and he was eager to learn more about it. "What do you mean?" he asked.

The spirit chuckled, and its eyes danced with amusement. "You'll see, Tom," it said. "Come back to the lake tomorrow, and I will show you something truly magical."

Sam was eager to return to the lake and discover the magic that the spirit had promised him. He arrived at the lake the next day, and he saw that the spirit was waiting for him.

The spirit led Sam to a small boat that was anchored at the edge of the lake. The boat was unlike anything Sam had ever seen before, and he was filled with a sense of wonder as he climbed aboard.

"Where are we going?" asked Tom, his voice filled with excitement.

The spirit smiled and gestured towards the center of the lake. "To the heart of the magic," it said.

As the boat glided across the water, Sam saw that the trees surrounding the lake were alive with magic. The branches were covered in shimmering leaves, and the trees seemed to be whispering secrets to each other.

The boat reached the center of the lake, and the spirit gestured towards a small island that was surrounded by a ring of fire.

"That is the heart of the magic," the spirit said. "And it is where you will find what you are looking for."

Sam looked at the island with awe and fear, and he wondered what he would find there. The spirit smiled at him, and its eyes twinkled.

"Don't be afraid," it said. "The magic will guide you."

Sam stepped off the boat and onto the island, and he saw that the fire was not burning at all. Instead, it was a ring of light that was beckoning him forward. He walked towards the light, and he felt a sense of wonder and joy fill his heart.

As Sam approached the heart of the magic, he saw that it was a tree that was unlike any other tree he had ever seen. The tree was tall and magnificent, and its branches were covered in golden leaves that glimmered in the light.

Sam reached out and touched one of the leaves, and he was amazed to see that it was solid gold. He couldn't believe his luck, and he was filled with excitement as he gathered as many leaves as he could carry.

Sam returned to the village with his treasure, and he was greeted with cheers and applause. The villagers were amazed by the gold leaves, and they were filled with gratitude towards Sam for bringing them such a gift.

Sam realized that the magic of the lake had given him a gift that was much greater than gold. He had found a new sense of wonder and joy, and he knew that he would cherish it forever.

And so, Sam lived the rest of his life with a smile on his face, and he was always eager to share his stories of the magic lake with anyone who would listen. The magic of the lake remained with him, and it always reminded him of the importance of friendship, courage, and wonder.

The end.

The Tale of the Super Tall Boy

Once upon a time, there was a boy named Ben who was unlike any other boy in the village. Ben was so tall that his head nearly touched the clouds, and the other children often teased him for his height.

Despite the teasing, Ben was a kind and gentle boy, and he never let the words of others hurt him. He was always curious about the world around him, and he loved to explore the forests and hills that surrounded the village.

One day, Ben was walking through the forest when he came across a wise old man who was sitting by a stream. The old man looked up and smiled at Ben, and Ben felt drawn to him.

"Good day, young man," said the old man. "What brings you to these parts?"

"I'm just exploring," said Ben, his eyes shining with excitement. "I love to see what's beyond the village."

The old man nodded and smiled. "You are a curious one, aren't you?" he said. "You remind me of someone I once knew."

"Really?" asked Ben, his eyes wide with surprise. "Who was that?"

The old man chuckled. "That is a story for another day," he said. "For now, let's just say that your height may be more of a blessing than you realize."

And with that, the old man bid Ben farewell, and Ben continued on his journey, filled with a sense of wonder and anticipation.

As Ben continued his journey, he encountered many obstacles and challenges. He met a giant who tried to scare him, but Ben's height and bravery allowed him to outwit the giant. He also encountered a dragon who breathed fire, but Ben's quick thinking and clever plan allowed him to defeat the dragon and save a princess who was trapped in a tower.

At every turn, Ben's height proved to be a blessing, and he gained more confidence in himself and his abilities. He continued on his journey, eager to see what other adventures lay ahead.

Eventually, Ben arrived at a castle that was surrounded by a moat of boiling lava. A wicked sorcerer lived in the castle, and he had taken control of the kingdom, ruling with an iron fist and spreading fear wherever he went.

Ben knew that he had to defeat the sorcerer if he wanted to restore peace to the kingdom. He approached the castle, his heart pounding with excitement and fear.

As Ben approached the castle, he was suddenly faced with a barrage of spells and curses from the sorcerer. But Ben stood firm, relying on his wit and bravery to protect himself.

Finally, the sorcerer launched a powerful spell that seemed to be heading straight for Ben. But Ben held out his hand, and the spell was absorbed into his palm. He then concentrated his power and sent a blast of energy back at the sorcerer, destroying him and freeing the kingdom from his grasp.

With the sorcerer defeated, Ben was hailed as a hero by the people of the kingdom. He was given a royal welcome, and he was showered with gifts and accolades. Ben was filled with joy and pride, knowing that his journey had led him to this moment of triumph.

As Ben settled into life as a hero, he started to realize that there was still much work to be done. The kingdom was in ruins, and the people were in need of help and support. Ben decided that he would stay and help the kingdom to rebuild and recover.

Over the next few months, Ben worked tirelessly to help the kingdom get back on its feet. He used his strength and wisdom to repair damaged buildings, sow crops, and clear forests. The people of the kingdom admired Ben's kindness and selflessness, and they began to see him as a true leader.

As the kingdom started to prosper, Ben realized that he had found a new home. He had made many friends and had been welcomed with open arms by the people of the kingdom. He knew that he would never leave this place, and that he would always be remembered as the boy who loved night and who had become a hero.

And so, Ben lived happily ever after, ruling the kingdom with justice and fairness, and always remembering the friends and adventures that had brought him to this place.

The end.

The Boy Who Loved to Dance

Once upon a time, there was a young boy named Nathan who lived in a small village. Nathan was different from the other boys in the village, for he loved to dance. He would spend hours practicing his steps and twirling about, lost in the rhythm of the music.

One day, Nathan was out in the woods, practicing his dance moves, when he came across an old woman. The old woman asked Nathan why he was dancing, and Nathan replied, "I love to dance! It makes me feel free and happy."

The old woman smiled and said, "Nathan, I have a task for you. There is a prince who has been cursed by a wicked fairy. The curse has taken away the prince's ability to dance, and he is in great despair. Only the touch of someone who truly loves to dance can break the curse and restore the prince's joy."

Nathan was filled with excitement. He knew that he had to help the prince and break the curse. He thanked the old woman and set off on his journey, eager to find the prince and help him dance again.

Nathan traveled far and wide, determined to find the prince and break the curse. He danced through forests, across rivers, and over mountains, never once losing his passion for the art.

As Nathan approached the prince's castle, he was met by a group of fierce guards. "What is your business here?" they demanded.

Nathan replied, "I have come to break the curse on the prince and restore his ability to dance."

The guards laughed, "You? Break the curse? That is impossible! No one has ever been able to break the curse. Leave now or face the consequences."

Nathan stood his ground, "I am not afraid. I will not leave until I have helped the prince."

The guards hesitated, then stepped aside, allowing Nathan to enter the castle. Nathan found the prince sitting in his throne room, looking sad and defeated.

Nathan approached the prince and said, "Your Highness, I have come to break the curse and restore your ability to dance."

The prince looked up at Nathan, hope in his eyes, "Is it truly possible? Can you break the curse?"

Nathan took the prince's hand and led him to the center of the room. He began to dance, twirling and leaping, his passion for the art shining bright.

As Nathan danced, the curse began to break. The prince started to move, his feet tapping in time with the music. And soon, the prince was dancing with Nathan, his joy and happiness restored.

The people of the kingdom cheered, and Nathan and the prince danced together, reveling in the joy of their shared love for dance.

After the prince's curse was broken, Nathan was hailed as a hero throughout the kingdom. The prince offered him any reward he desired, but Nathan declined, saying that the joy of dance was reward enough.

Nathan continued to dance, spreading joy and happiness wherever he went. And the prince, no longer cursed, became a great dancer in his own right. They remained friends, always dancing together whenever they had the chance.

And as for the kingdom, it became a place of happiness, where music and dance flourished. The people of the kingdom danced and sang, grateful for the gift that Nathan had brought them. And they all lived happily ever after.

The end.

The Three Brave Girls and the Magic Maze

Once upon a time, in a kingdom far away, there lived three sisters named Emily, Mia, and Ava. They lived in a small cottage with their parents, who were poor but loving. Emily, Mia, and Ava were known throughout the kingdom for their bravery, kindness, and intelligence.

One day, the king of the kingdom announced that he had built a magic maze, and whoever solved it would receive a great reward. The girls were intrigued and decided to try their luck.

At the entrance of the maze, the girls encountered a mysterious old man who told them: "Beware, for the maze is full of tricks and dangers. But if you have courage in your hearts, and you work together, you will reach the end and find the greatest treasure of all."

And so, the girls entered the maze, determined to solve its mysteries and find the treasure.

Emily: This maze is so confusing. I don't know which way to turn.

Mia: Let's stick together and keep our eyes open. We can do this!

Ava: We have each other, and that's the most important thing. We'll find the treasure together.

And so, the three brave girls embarked on their journey through the magic maze, facing challenges and solving puzzles along the way. But they never lost sight of their goal, and their courage and determination saw them through.

As the girls continued through the maze, they encountered more and more challenges. At one point, they came across a room with a deep pit in the center.

Emily: How are we going to get across this pit?

Mia: I have an idea. We can use these ropes to swing across.

Ava: But what if the ropes break?

Emily: We must trust each other and have faith in ourselves. We can do this.

And so, the girls swung across the pit, one by one, holding onto the ropes tightly. They made it safely to the other side, and the maze continued.

At another point, the girls found themselves in a room filled with mirrors, and they couldn't tell which way to go.

Ava: Which way is the right way?

Mia: We need to use our intelligence to figure this out.

Emily: Let's look for any clues or patterns in the mirrors.

And so, the girls worked together to find the right path, using their wits and ingenuity. They finally found the way out of the room, and the maze continued.

Finally, the girls reached the end of the maze and found themselves in a large, glittering room filled with treasure. But in the center of the room stood a figure shrouded in shadows.

Ava: Who are you?

Mysterious figure: I am the keeper of the maze, and I have been watching you as you made your way through.

Emily: Why did you build this maze?

Keeper: I built the maze to find the bravest and most deserving individuals in the kingdom, for they are the only ones worthy of the treasure. And you, the three brave girls, have proven yourselves to be exactly that.

Mia: What is the greatest treasure of all?

Keeper: The greatest treasure of all is the knowledge and understanding that you have gained through your journey. You have learned to trust, to have faith, and to work together. And those are treasures that no amount of gold or jewels can match.

And with that, the girls understood the true value of what they had accomplished, and they left the maze filled with joy and pride in their hearts.

The girls returned to the kingdom, where they were greeted as heroes. They told the king of their journey through the maze and of the treasure they had found.

King: You have done a great thing, and the kingdom is proud of you.

Emily: Thank you, your majesty. But the true treasure was what we learned along the way.

Ava: We learned the importance of trust, faith, and teamwork.

Mia: And those are the treasures that will stay with us forever.

The king was deeply moved by the girls' words, and he realized the true value of what they had accomplished. He decided to build a monument to their bravery, and the monument stood as a symbol of courage and determination for generations to come.

The girls continued to live their lives, but they never forgot their journey through the magic maze. They remained close friends and continued to work together, using the lessons they had learned to help others and make the world a better place.

The end.

The Sleepy Bear and the Annoying Snake

Once upon a time, in a peaceful and lush forest, there lived a big and cuddly bear named Bernie. Bernie was known for his love of napping, and he would often spend hours and hours sleeping, curled up in his cozy den.

One day, while Bernie was in the middle of a nap, an annoying little snake slithered into his den. The snake was always looking for attention and would often play pranks on the other animals in the forest.

Snake: "Hey there, sleepy bear! Wake up! It's time to play!"

Bear: "What? Go away! I'm trying to sleep!"

Snake: "Sleep? That's no fun! Come on, let's play hide and seek! I'll count, and you hide!"

Bear: "I said, go away! I just want to sleep!"

But the snake was not easily deterred, and he continued to pester the bear, trying to get him to play. The bear, becoming increasingly irritated, tried to ignore the snake and get back to his nap. But the snake's constant chattering and pranks made it impossible for the bear to sleep.

And so, the stage was set for a battle of wits and determination between the sleepy bear and the annoying snake.

The snake continued to annoy the bear, day in and day out, and the bear became more and more frustrated with the snake's behavior. Finally, one day, the bear had had enough.

Bear: "Listen here, snake. I've had enough of your antics. I just want to sleep in peace."

Snake: "Ha! You're no fun, bear. What's the point of being awake if you're not going to play and have fun?"

Bear: "The point is, I need my sleep. It's essential for my health and wellbeing. And I won't let you or anyone else take that away from me."

And so, the bear challenged the snake to a contest to see who could stay awake the longest. The snake, always up for a challenge, accepted.

The contest began, and the bear and the snake both tried their best to stay awake. The snake tried to distract the bear with jokes and pranks, but the bear was determined to win. He focused all his energy on staying awake and refused to give in to the temptation of sleep.

As the hours went by, the snake began to tire and nod off, but the bear refused to give up. Finally, after what seemed like an eternity, the snake let out a loud snore, and the contest was over. The bear had won!

Bear: "Ha! I told you I was determined to win. And now, if you'll excuse me, I think I'll take that nap I've been craving."

From that day on, the snake learned to respect the bear's need for sleep and to understand the importance of rest and rejuvenation. The bear, in turn, became more patient and understanding towards the snake's playful nature.

The two animals became fast friends and would often be seen playing together and exploring the forest. They learned to appreciate each other's strengths and to see each other in a new light.

And so, the story of the sleepy bear and the annoying snake became a beloved tale, told, and retold by the animals of the forest. It served as a reminder of the importance of respect and understanding, and how two vastly different creatures can become the best of friends if they are willing to learn from each other and appreciate each other's differences.

And whenever the animals of the forest encountered someone who was too stubborn to see the other side of the story, they would tell the tale of the bear and the snake, and how they learned to live in harmony despite their differences. And the other animals would listen, and they too would learn the importance of respect and understanding, and they would strive to live in peace and harmony with each other, just like the bear and the snake.

The end.

The Brave Mouse of the Castle

Once upon a time, in a kingdom far, far away, there lived a small mouse named David. David lived in a cozy mouse hole in the castle walls and spent his days gathering crumbs from the banquet table and playing with his mouse friends.

One day, as David was exploring the castle, he stumbled upon a secret passage. Intrigued, he followed the passage until he came to a room filled with treasure. But as he was admiring the gold and jewels, he heard a loud noise. Suddenly, the door to the room slammed shut, trapping David inside.

David was scared, but he knew he had to find a way out. He searched the room, but all the doors were locked tight. Suddenly, he heard a voice. It was the voice of the castle's guardian, a fierce dragon.

"Who dares to intrude upon my treasure? Show yourself, small mouse!"

David trembled with fear, but he mustered up the courage to speak.

"It's just me, David the mouse. I didn't mean to cause any trouble. I was just exploring the castle and stumbled upon this room by accident."

"Ha! An intruder and a liar. You will never leave this room alive. But first, I shall play a game with you. I will ask you three riddles, and if you can answer all three correctly, I shall set you free."

David's heart sank. He was a mouse, not a riddle master. But he knew he had to try. He took a deep breath and prepared to face the dragon's riddles.

"First riddle. What is always in front of you but can't be seen?"

David thought for a moment and then answered confidently.

"The future."

"Correct. Second riddle. What is always behind you but can't be touched?"

David thought for a moment and then answered confidently.

"The past."

"Correct. Third riddle. What is alive that doesn't heartbeat?"

David thought for a long time, but he couldn't come up with an answer. The dragon's roar filled the room, and David cowered in fear.

Just then, David remembered a saying his mother used to tell him when he was a baby mouse: "The answer to every riddle lies within your heart." David closed his eyes and took a deep breath. He remembered all the adventures he'd had with his mouse friends and the bravery he'd shown in facing danger. And then he knew the answer.

"A plant."

"Correct! I am impressed, small mouse. You have a wise and brave heart. I release you from my riddles."

David's heart lifted with joy as the dragon breathed fire onto the treasure room door, melting the lock and allowing David to escape.

David ran as fast as he could back to the castle's main hall, where the king and queen were waiting for him. When they saw David, they ran over to him, overjoyed that he had escaped from the dragon and solved its riddles.

King asked, "David, you are truly a hero! How did you manage to escape the dragon and solve its riddles?"

David replied, "I remembered a saying my mother used to tell me when I was a baby mouse: 'The answer to every riddle lies within your heart.' I closed my eyes and took a deep breath. I remembered all the adventures I'd had with my mouse friends and the bravery I'd shown in facing danger. And then I knew the answer."

Queen nodded, "You have shown remarkable bravery and wit, David. We are proud to call you one of our own. From this day forward, you will be known as the bravest mouse in all the kingdom."

David smiled, feeling proud and grateful for the recognition he was receiving. He knew he would never forget this adventure, and he would always be ready for the next one.

And so, David settled back into life at the castle, but now he was even more beloved by the king and queen, and all the other mice, for his bravery and cleverness. He continued to go on adventures and solve riddles, always using his quick wit and bravery to protect his friends and family. And he lived happily ever after, always ready for his next adventure.

The end.

The Girl Who Loved Flowers

Once upon a time, in a kingdom surrounded by rolling hills and lush gardens, there lived a girl named Rosie. Rosie was known throughout the kingdom for her love of flowers. She could often be found tending to the gardens and arranging bouquets of blooms, her eyes sparkling with joy.

Rosie: "Flowers have a magic all their own, you know. Each petal, each fragrance, holds a story just waiting to be told."

One day, while exploring the gardens, Rosie stumbled upon a hidden meadow filled with the most beautiful flowers she had ever seen. Each bloom was more vibrant and fragrant than the last, and Rosie couldn't help but be drawn to them.

Rosie: "Oh, what a magical place! I must come here every day to learn from these flowers and find the stories they have to tell."

And so, Rosie made the hidden meadow her secret garden, spending hours there every day, learning about the different flowers and the tales they held. She became known as the girl who loved flowers, and her reputation for creating the most beautiful bouquets in the kingdom grew.

But Rosie little know, the hidden meadow held a secret that would change her life forever.

One day, Rosie discovered that the flowers in the hidden meadow were starting to wilt and die. She was heartbroken and couldn't understand why this was happening.

Rosie: "What's happening to my beloved flowers? They're the source of my joy and inspiration, and now they're dying right before my eyes."

Rosie soon learned that a wicked witch, who lived on the outskirts of the kingdom, was behind the destruction of the flowers. The witch had become jealous of the beauty and magic that the flowers held, and so she cast a spell that was slowly killing them all.

Rosie: "I have to do something. I can't let the witch destroy my beloved flowers and the magic they hold."

Determined to save the flowers, Rosie set out on a journey to find the wicked witch. Along the way, she met many challenges and obstacles, but she didn't give up. She was determined to save the flowers and restore their magic.

Finally, after many days of travel, Rosie arrived at the witch's lair. The witch was powerful and cruel, but Rosie was brave and refused to be intimidated.

Rosie: "I've come to stop you from destroying the magic of the flowers. I won't let you take away their beauty and their stories."

Despite the witch's power, Rosie's love and determination proved to be stronger. With her bravery and quick thinking, Rosie was able to break the spell and restore the magic to the flowers.

The witch was defeated, and the flowers in the hidden meadow bloomed once more, their colors more vibrant and fragrant than ever before.

Rosie returned to the kingdom as a hero, and the people celebrated her bravery and love of flowers. From that day forward, the hidden meadow became a place of pilgrimage for all who sought to learn from the flowers and discover their magic.

Rosie continued to create the most beautiful bouquets in the kingdom and inspire others to appreciate the beauty and magic of flowers. And she lived happily ever after, surrounded by the flowers she loved so much.

Rosie: "Flowers may be delicate, but their magic is strong. They remind us to never give up on our dreams and to always follow our hearts."

The end.

The Fastest Boy in the Kingdom

Once upon a time, there lived a young boy named Oliver who loved nothing more than to run. He ran everywhere he went, and he was always the first one to finish any race he entered. Everyone in the kingdom knew him as the fastest boy around.

One day, Oliver decided he wanted to enter the annual running competition that took place in the kingdom's capital city. It was the biggest race of the year, and the winner would be crowned the fastest runner in the kingdom.

Oliver's friends tried to talk him out of it, telling him that the competition was for grown-ups, not kids like him. But Oliver was determined. He knew he was the fastest runner in the kingdom, and he was going to prove it.

Oliver said, "I've been training for this race for months. I know I can win it!"

A friend of Oliver advised, "Oliver, the competition is fierce. You'll be up against some of the best runners in the kingdom. Are you sure you want to do this?"

Oliver nodded, "I'm positive! I'm not afraid of a little competition. I know I can beat them all!"

And with that, Oliver set off for the capital city, ready to take on the best runners in the kingdom and prove once and for all that he was the fastest boy in the land.

Oliver arrived at the capital city and met the other runners, all of whom were much older and bigger than he was. But Oliver didn't let that get to him. He was confident in his abilities and knew that he could beat them all.

The day of the race arrived, and Oliver lined up at the starting line with the other runners. The gun went off, and they were off, running as fast as they could. Oliver was running neck and neck with the other runners, determined to win.

As they approached the finish line, it looked like the winner would be a close call between Oliver and one of the other runners. But then, something miraculous happened. Oliver's legs started to move faster and faster, and he zoomed past the other runners, crossing the finish line first.

Crowd shouted, "The winner is Oliver! Oliver is the fastest runner in the kingdom!"

Oliver replied, "I did it! I won!"

Oliver was overjoyed. He had proved his friends wrong and shown the kingdom that he was indeed the fastest boy in the land.

But then, something unexpected happened. One of the other runners approached him, hand extended.

One of the runners celebrated, "Oliver, I have to admit, I'm impressed. You're a fantastic runner. You deserved to win today."

Oliver was taken aback. He had expected the other runners to be angry with him for winning, not to congratulate him.

One of the runners said, "I know I may not look like it, but I used to be just like you, full of energy and love for running. But as we grow older, we lose that spark. You've reminded me of why I started running in the first place. Thank you."

Oliver replied, "No, thank you. You've taught me a valuable lesson. Running isn't just about winning, it's about the joy of the race."

And from that day on, Oliver ran not just to win, but to find joy in every step of the journey. The crowd erupted in applause, and Oliver was hailed as the fastest runner in the land. From that day on, he and the runners became great friends and trained together, pushing each other to become even faster.

And so, Oliver learned that true friendship is about supporting each other and striving for excellence, not about winning or losing. And he lived happily ever after, always running and always making new friends along the way.

The end.

The Lonely Star

Once upon a time, in a far-off galaxy, there was a star named Twinkle. Twinkle was a bright and shining star, known throughout the universe for its beauty and brilliance. But despite its fame and fortune, Twinkle was feeling lonely.

You see, Twinkle was the only star in its corner of the galaxy, and it had no friends to talk to or play with. Day after day, Twinkle would shine brightly, illuminating the dark void of space, but it always felt like something was missing.

One day, as Twinkle was shining its brightest, it suddenly spoke up.

Twinkle: "Is there anyone out there? I am feeling so lonely, and I would like a friend to talk to."

There was silence for a moment, and then, from the darkness, a voice spoke up.

Voice: "I am here, Twinkle. I am a planet, and I would be happy to be your friend."

Twinkle was overjoyed to have found a friend, and it eagerly asked the planet what it was like.

Planet: "I am a rocky planet, with mountains and valleys, rivers and oceans. I orbit around my star, just as you orbit around yours. But I too am lonely, as I have no other planets to talk to or play with."

Twinkle was pleased to hear that it was not alone in its feelings of loneliness, and it agreed to be the planet's friend.

And so, the stage was set for a friendship between Twinkle the star and the lonely planet, as they set out to explore the universe and discover all its wonders.

Twinkle and the planet became fast friends, sharing stories and experiences as they traveled through the universe. They explored galaxies and marveled at the beauty of the stars, watching as they danced and twinkled in the night sky.

One day, as they were flying through a particularly dark corner of the universe, they came upon a strange and dangerous place. The stars were all dying, one by one, and the darkness was spreading like a disease.

Twinkle: "What is happening here, Planet? Why are all the stars dying?"

Planet: "I don't know, Twinkle. But it's clear that something is wrong, and we must find out what it is."

Twinkle: "But what can we do? We are just one star and one planet. How can we stop this darkness?"

Planet: "We may be small, Twinkle, but we have something even more powerful than size. We have our friendship. Together, I know we can do anything."

And with that, Twinkle and the planet set out to uncover the cause of the darkness, determined to save the stars and bring light back to the universe.

Twinkle and the planet traveled deep into the heart of the darkness, their courage and friendship guiding them every step of the way. They discovered that the source of the darkness was a black hole, which was sucking in all the stars and destroying them.

Twinkle and the planet knew that they had to act quickly, but they also knew that they could not face the black hole alone. So, they called out to all the other stars and planets in the universe, asking for their help in defeating the darkness.

To their surprise, stars and planets from all over the universe answered their call, coming together to form a magnificent array of light and energy. Together, they formed a beam of light that was so bright and powerful that it reached all the way to the black hole and pushed it away, saving the stars and defeating the darkness once and for all.

With the black hole defeated, the stars and planets all rejoiced, their light shining brightly in the universe once again. And Twinkle and the planet, proud and happy, knew that they had saved the universe and brought back the light, all thanks to their friendship and the power of working together.

From that day on, Twinkle and the planet remained the best of friends, their friendship shining brighter than any star in the sky. And they were a reminder to all the creatures of the universe that, no matter how small or insignificant they may seem, they have the power to make a difference, so long as they have the courage to try and the strength of friendship to guide them.

The end.

The Ugly Magic Shoes

Once upon a time, there was a young boy named Ivan who lived in a small village at the edge of a vast and mysterious forest. Ivan was a kind and curious boy, always eager to explore the world and learn new things.

One day, Ivan stumbled upon an old, worn-out pair of shoes lying in the dirt. They were unlike any shoes he had ever seen before - they were made of a strange, shimmering material, and they seemed to glow with a magical light.

Ivan picked up the shoes and put them on, and as soon as he did, he felt a strange energy coursing through his body. He took a step, and to his surprise, the shoes began to move of their own accord, carrying him further into the forest.

Ivan felt a sense of excitement and wonder as he was carried deeper into the forest, his feet moving faster and faster, until he finally came to a stop in a small clearing.

In the center of the clearing stood an old man, dressed in a long, flowing cloak. The old man approached Ivan and looked down at the shoes on his feet.

The old man said, "Ah, the magic shoes. I have been searching for those for many years. They have the power to grant the wearer their greatest wish, but they also come with a curse."

Ivan was shocked, and he looked down at the shoes on his feet. They were certainly magical, but they were also the ugliest things he had ever seen. He wondered if the power they held was worth the curse that came with them.

Ivan was torn about the shoes - he wanted the power they held, but he didn't want to be cursed. But as he continued to wear the shoes, he began to notice that they were changing. They were growing bigger and uglier, until they looked like giant, clunky monstrosities on his feet.

Ivan was horrified. He couldn't walk around in public with such ugly shoes, and he felt like everyone was staring at him. He tried to take the shoes off, but he found that he couldn't. They were stuck to his feet, and he was stuck with the curse.

Ivan felt like his life was over. He was ashamed of the shoes, and he was sure that everyone was laughing at him. But as he was walking through the village one day, he saw a young girl who was crying.

The girl said, "My father is very sick, and the only thing that can save him is a rare flower that grows in the heart of the forest. But I'm afraid to go into the forest by myself, because it's full of danger."

Ivan felt a sense of purpose. He had the magic shoes, and he was brave enough to go into the forest and find the flower. He decided to help the girl, and he set off into the forest, the ugly magic shoes leading the way.

As Ivan and the girl made their way deeper into the forest, they encountered all sorts of dangers - fierce beasts, treacherous terrain, and more. But Ivan was determined to save the girl's father, and he used the magic shoes to guide him through each obstacle.

Finally, they arrived at the heart of the forest, where the rare flower grew. Ivan plucked the flower and gave it to the girl, and together they set off back to the village.

But as they were making their way back, they heard a loud roar echoing through the forest. They turned to see a massive dragon, its eyes glowing with fire, coming straight at them.

Ivan knew that they had to act fast. He grabbed the girl and used the magic shoes to jump up into the air, soaring over the dragon's head and landing safely on the other side.

Ivan and the girl returned to the village, where they were greeted with cheers and applause. The girl's father was given the rare flower, and he was quickly healed.

Ivan was hailed as a hero, and he was amazed at how the ugly magic shoes had helped him to save the day. He began to realize that the curse of the shoes wasn't so bad after all, and that the power they held was worth the price he had paid.

In the end, Ivan decided to keep the shoes. He knew that they would always be with him, guiding him through whatever dangers he might face. And he was happy to have the power to help others, to be a hero whenever he was needed.

The girl and her father became good friends with Ivan, and they all lived happily ever after. And whenever Ivan needed to be reminded of the magic of the shoes, all he had to do was look down at his feet, and he knew that he was never alone.

The end.

The Boy and the Underwater Kingdom

Once upon a time, there was a young boy named Andres who lived near the sea. He loved to spend his days exploring the shore and learning about the creatures that lived in the sea.

One day, as Andres was swimming in the sea, he stumbled upon a strange, glowing shell. He picked it up and was amazed to see that it was actually a magical conch shell. Andres held the conch shell to his ear and was surprised to hear a voice calling out to him.

"Andres," the voice said. "I am the king of the underwater kingdom. I need your help to defeat a great evil that is threatening our home."

Andres was stunned. He had never heard of an underwater kingdom before, and he was eager to learn more.

"What can I do to help?" Andres asked the voice.

"Come to the underwater kingdom and meet with me," the voice replied. "I will give you all the information you need to save our home."

Andres was excited and a little bit scared, but he knew he had to help. He put on his diving gear and swam down into the depths of the sea, eager to begin his underwater adventure.

Andres swam deeper and deeper into the sea, and soon he saw a large, beautiful castle made of coral and pearls. He swam towards it and was greeted by the king of the underwater kingdom.

"Thank you for coming, Andres," the king said. "We are in grave danger. An evil octopus named Kraken has been terrorizing our kingdom, stealing our treasure and destroying our homes."

Andres was horrified. He had never heard of such a powerful and wicked creature. But he was determined to help the king and his kingdom.

"What can I do?" Andres asked.

"We need you to retrieve the Lost Trident, a powerful weapon that has the power to defeat Kraken," the king replied. "But it is guarded by many dangers and traps, and only a brave adventurer like yourself can retrieve it."

Andres was ready for the challenge. He set out on his quest, swimming through the treacherous waters and overcoming many obstacles. He battled giant squid and dodged schools of piranhas, determined to retrieve the Lost Trident and save the underwater kingdom.

Andres finally reached the location of the Lost Trident, and he was amazed to see its beauty and power. But just as he was about to reach for it, he was confronted by Kraken, the evil octopus.

"Ha!" Kraken laughed. "You think you can defeat me with that trident? I am the ruler of the sea, and you are nothing but a mere mortal."

Andres was scared, but he knew he had to fight for the sake of the underwater kingdom. He bravely stood his ground and prepared for battle. The two clashed in an epic fight, their powers battling against each other. Just when it seemed like Andres might not win, he remembered the words of the king, "The Lost Trident is powerful, but only a brave heart can truly wield its strength."

With a newfound courage, Andres used the trident to defeat Kraken and save the underwater kingdom. The kingdom cheered and celebrated their victory, and Andres was hailed as a hero.

After defeating Kraken and saving the underwater kingdom, Andres returned to the king with the Lost Trident. The king was overjoyed and grateful, and he offered Andres anything he desired as a reward.

Andres thought for a moment and then spoke. "Your majesty, I have everything I need. I have made many new friends, and I have had the adventure of a lifetime. The greatest reward would be to continue exploring the sea and discovering new wonders."

The king smiled. "Very well, Andres. You may explore the sea as much as you like. And remember, you are always welcome here in the underwater kingdom."

Andres continued to explore the sea, discovering new wonders and making new friends. He never forgot the bravery and determination he showed in defeating Kraken and saving the underwater kingdom, and he lived a happy and adventurous life as a hero of the sea.

The end.

The Mysterious Island

Once upon a time, there were two best friends named Tavy and Luke who loved to go on adventures together. They lived near a large lake and often spent their days fishing and exploring its shores.

One day, while they were fishing, they noticed something strange. Far out in the middle of the lake, there was a small island that they had never seen before. They decided to row out to the island to explore.

When they arrived, they were amazed at what they saw. The island was covered in lush vegetation and teemed with strange and exotic creatures they had never seen before. As they explored further, they found a hidden cave in the center of the island. They entered the cave and found a large, glittering treasure chest.

"Wow," said Tavy. "We've hit the Jackpot!"

"But what's inside?" asked Luke.

"There's only one way to find out," replied Tavy, opening the chest.

The two friends were stunned to find a beautiful golden key inside. They had no idea what it was for, but they felt like it must be important. They decided to take the key back to the mainland and try to find out what it was for. Little did they know, their adventure was just beginning.

Tavy and Luke brought the key to the local wise man, hoping he could shed some light on its purpose. The wise man took one look at the key and gasped.

"This is the key to the treasure of the lake!" he exclaimed. "It's said to be guarded by a powerful monster, but whoever finds the key and unlocks the treasure will be granted unlimited wealth and happiness."

Excited by the prospect of unlimited wealth, Tavy and Luke set out on a mission to find the treasure. They rowed back to the island and explored its many caves and crevices, determined to find the treasure and the monster that guarded it.

As they searched, they encountered all sorts of obstacles and danger, but they refused to give up. Finally, they stumbled upon a dark and ominous cavern. At the back of the cavern, they saw a large, glittering treasure chest surrounded by a fierce monster.

Tavy and Luke stood frozen, not knowing what to do. The monster was enormous and incredibly fierce, but they were determined to unlock the treasure. Tavy stepped forward, key in hand.

"We've come for the treasure," he said, trying to sound brave.

The monster roared in response, but Tavy refused to back down. With a shaking hand, he inserted the key into the lock and turned it. The chest creaked open, and the monster let out a final roar before collapsing to the ground.

Tavy and Luke cautiously approached the treasure chest and peered inside. It was filled with gold, diamonds, and precious gems of all shapes and sizes. They looked at each other in amazement, their wildest dreams finally coming true.

With the treasure in hand, Tavy and Luke knew they needed to leave the island and return home. They packed as much of the treasure as they could carry and set out for home, eager to share their good fortune with their families.

As they journeyed back, they encountered many challenges and obstacles, but they were able to overcome them all with their newfound wealth and bravery. When they finally returned home, their families were overjoyed to see them and hear about their incredible adventure.

Tavy and Luke divided the treasure among their families, making sure everyone was taken care of. They used their wealth to help those in need and to build a better life for themselves and their loved ones.

Tavy and Luke known as the two brave boys who had unlocked the treasure of the lake and brought back unlimited wealth and happiness. They lived long, happy lives, and the story of their adventure was inspiring many young boys to follow in their footsteps and seek out their own adventures.

The end.

The Sweet House

Once upon a time, there was a village where all the houses were made of brick, stone, and wood. But there was one house that stood out from the rest. It was a house made of sweets.

The house was made of gingerbread, chocolate, and other sugary treats. It was a beautiful sight to see, with icing in all different colors and candies in all shapes and sizes decorating the exterior.

The owner of the house was a little girl named Lily. She loved sweets and she loved to bake. She had built the house herself, using her baking skills to create a home made entirely of sweets.

Lily was proud of her house and she loved to show it off to anyone who came to visit. She would often invite her friends over and they would spend hours admiring the house and trying different sweets.

But one day, a group of children came to the village and they weren't like any children the village had seen before. They were mean and mischievous, and they loved to play tricks on the other children.

When they saw Lily's sweet house, they knew they had found the perfect target. They began to throw stones at the house, breaking off chunks of gingerbread and shattering pieces of candy. Lily was heartbroken, watching as her beautiful house was destroyed before her eyes.

Lily was devastated by the destruction of her sweet house. She didn't know what to do. She was about to give up when she remembered all the love and care she had put into building her house. She realized that the house wasn't just made of sweets, it was made of her love and creativity.

She decided that she wasn't going to let the mean children win. She started to rebuild her house, using all the sweets she had left. She worked tirelessly, day and night, until the house was restored to its former glory.

As she finished, she stepped back and admired her work. She was proud of what she had accomplished, and she knew that the house was stronger now than it had ever been before.

Lily: "I won't let anyone break my spirit. This house is a symbol of my love and creativity, and it's stronger than ever now."

Word of Lily's sweet house spread quickly throughout the village, and people started coming from far and wide to see it. They were amazed at her determination and her creativity, and they admired her for her strength.

The mean children were ashamed of what they had done, and they asked Lily for forgiveness. They realized that their actions had only made her house stronger, and they admired her for her resilience.

Lily forgave the mean children and she welcomed them into her home, showing them her sweets and her love. They became her friends, and they would often visit her and help her with her baking.

Lily's sweet house became a place of happiness and love, and everyone in the village was proud of her and her creation. She became known as the Sweet Baker, and her house became a place of joy and inspiration for generations to come.

Lily: "I learned that love and creativity are the strongest forces in the world. And my house, made of sweets, is a testament to that love and creativity."

The end.

The Lucky Ring

Once upon a time, there was a young boy named Kait who lived in a small village. Kait was a kind and hardworking boy, but he often felt like he was destined for something more. One day, Kait stumbled upon an old ring lying on the ground. He picked it up and, to his surprise, the ring was glowing with a soft, warm light.

As Kait looked at the ring, he heard a voice speak to him. "Kait, I am a lucky ring," the voice said. "I can grant you anything you desire, but you must use my power wisely."

Kait was amazed and a little afraid, but he knew that this was the opportunity he had been waiting for. "I want to go on an adventure," he said.

"Very well," said the voice. "The adventure awaits you. Just remember, choose wisely."

And with that, Kait set off on his greatest adventure, with the lucky ring guiding him every step of the way.

Kait traveled far and wide, using the lucky ring's powers to overcome obstacles and achieve his goals. Everywhere he went, he helped people in need and made new friends.

One day, Kait heard about a terrible dragon that was terrorizing a nearby kingdom. The dragon was said to be nearly invincible, and no one had been able to defeat it.

But Kait was not afraid. He had the lucky ring, and he knew that with its help, he could defeat the dragon and save the kingdom.

When Kait arrived at the kingdom, he was greeted by the king, who was desperate for help. "Please, Kait," said the king. "The dragon is destroying everything in its path. We need your help to defeat it."

Kait nodded. "I'll do my best," he said.

With the lucky ring's guidance, Kait set out to find the dragon. When he finally came face-to-face with the beast, it was even more terrifying than he had imagined. The dragon breathed fire, and its eyes glowed with a wicked light.

But Kait was determined. He drew his sword and charged forward, determined to defeat the dragon and save the kingdom.

As he fought the dragon, Kait remembered the voice of the lucky ring. "Choose wisely," it had said. And Kait knew exactly what he had to do. He sheathed his sword and approached the dragon slowly and cautiously.

"Dragon," he said. "I know you are just acting out of fear and anger. But I have come to help you. Let me help you find peace."

The dragon looked at Kait with surprise, and then it lowered its head. "I don't know how," it said. "I have never known anything but fear and anger."

"I can help you," said Kait. "I will be your friend."

And with that, Kait and the dragon began their journey towards peace and friendship.

As Kait and the dragon traveled together, they encountered many challenges and obstacles. But with Kait's kindness and the power of the lucky ring, they were able to overcome them all.

The dragon learned to trust Kait and began to open up to him. It shared with Kait its deepest fears and desires, and Kait listened and offered comfort and support.

Together, Kait and the dragon explored the kingdom, making friends with the people and animals they met along the way. The dragon's reputation as a fearsome beast slowly faded, and it was replaced by a reputation of a kind and gentle creature.

Eventually, Kait and the dragon returned to the kingdom. The people were amazed at the transformation in the dragon, and they hailed Kait as a hero.

The king, who had once been so desperate for help, thanked Kait for his bravery and for showing the dragon a different way of living.

And Kait, who had once been an ordinary boy, now realized that with the lucky ring and the dragon by his side, he could achieve anything he set his mind to. He knew that the journey towards peace and happiness would never truly be over, but he was grateful for the friends and adventures he had made along the way.

The end.

The Brave Boy and the Scary Cave

Once upon a time, there was a brave young boy named Richard who lived in a small village at the edge of a vast and mysterious forest. Richard was always eager for adventure and was never afraid of anything, no matter how dangerous or frightening it may be.

One day, Richard heard the villagers talking about a dark and mysterious cave that lay deep within the forest. They said that the cave was haunted by all manner of frightening creatures and that it was impossible to reach the bottom alive. But Richard was determined to explore the cave and discover what secrets lay within.

So, he gathered his courage and set off into the forest. He walked for hours, navigating through the dense trees and over the rough terrain, until he finally arrived at the entrance to the cave.

Richard stood at the entrance, looking into the darkness. He could hear strange sounds echoing from within, and he felt a chill run down his spine. But he was a brave boy, and he took a deep breath and stepped inside.

As he made his way deeper into the cave, he felt the walls closing in around him and the darkness growing thicker. He began to see strange shapes in the shadows and to hear strange whispers on the wind. But still, he pressed on, determined to reach the bottom and uncover the secrets of the cave.

Richard continued to explore the cave, his heart racing with excitement and fear. He encountered all sorts of strange and terrifying creatures, but he used his wits and bravery to outsmart them and escape their clutches.

As he neared the bottom of the cave, he came across a deep chasm. He could see a faint light far below, and he knew that he was close to his goal. He carefully made his way across the chasm, jumping from one narrow ledge to the next.

Finally, he reached the bottom of the cave and came across a door. It was old and rusted, but it was the only way to access the inner chamber. Richard tried to open the door, but it would not budge. He pushed and pulled with all his might, but it seemed to be stuck fast.

Just as Richard was about to give up hope, he heard a faint whisper. It was a voice, coming from the door itself.

"Who seeks to enter the inner chamber?" the voice asked.

"It is I, Richard," he replied. "I have come to explore the cave and uncover its secrets."

"Ah," the voice said. "You are brave, but you are also foolish. A powerful magic is guarding the inner chamber that only the bravest and wisest may penetrate. Are you brave enough to face this challenge?"

Richard took a deep breath and steeled himself for the task ahead. "I am," he said. "I will face whatever danger lies within."

And with that, the door creaked open, revealing a dimly lit chamber beyond. Richard stepped inside, his heart pounding with excitement and fear. What lay ahead, he did not know, but he was determined to face it with bravery and resolve.

Richard stepped inside the inner chamber and was immediately struck by the grandeur and beauty of the room. It was filled with sparkling gems and glittering gold, but what caught Richard's attention was a large, glowing crystal in the center of the room.

As Richard approached the crystal, he could feel a powerful magic radiating from it. He reached out to touch the crystal, and suddenly he was enveloped in a bright light. When the light faded, he found himself standing before a wise old wizard.

"Ah, Richard," the wizard said with a smile. "You have proven yourself to be a true hero. You have braved the dangers of the cave and faced the trials within, and now you have earned the reward."

The wizard then presented Richard with a magical pair of socks that would allow him to be strong.

Richard was overjoyed and thanked the wizard for the gift. He put on the socks and took to the air, soaring above the cave and feeling the rush of wind through his hair. He explored the skies and visited far-off lands, using his new magic socks to travel wherever he wanted. And although he had many more adventures, Richard never forgot the lessons he learned in the scary cave. He used his bravery and wisdom to help others and to continue to explore the world and uncover its many mysteries.

The end.

The Three Magic Rings

Once upon a time, in a kingdom far, far away, there lived a young girl named Rosalind. She was a kind and curious girl who loved to explore the world around her.

One day, as she was walking through the forest, she came across a small clearing where she found a box lying on the ground. She picked it up and opened it to find three beautiful rings inside.

Rosalind: "Oh, what beautiful rings! I wonder what they do?"

As she picked up the first ring, she heard a voice in her head.

Voice: "This is the ring of courage. It will give you the bravery to face any challenge."

Rosalind picked up the second ring and heard another voice.

Voice: "This is the ring of wisdom. It will give you the knowledge to make the right decisions."

Finally, she picked up the third ring and heard a third voice.

Voice: "This is the ring of love. It will give you the power to spread love and kindness wherever you go."

Rosalind was amazed by the rings and couldn't wait to explore the kingdom and see what kind of adventures they would lead her on. She put the rings on her fingers and set off on her journey, eager to see what lay ahead.

As Rosalind traveled through the kingdom, she discovered that the rings were more powerful than she could have ever imagined. With the ring of courage, she faced and overcame many challenges, from crossing treacherous rivers to scaling tall mountains.

With the ring of wisdom, she made wise decisions and solved many problems that the people of the kingdom faced. And with the ring of love, she spread kindness and love wherever she went, bringing happiness and hope to those who had lost it.

People started to take notice of Rosalind and her incredible powers, and they began to spread the word about her and her magical rings. Soon, the kingdom was buzzing with excitement, and many people set out to find her and ask for her help.

As Rosalind continued her journey, she eventually came across a powerful sorceress who was using her magic to terrorize the kingdom. The sorceress was determined to take the rings from Rosalind, believing that they would give her even greater power.

Rosalind stood her ground, determined to protect the rings and their powers. The sorceress tried to use her magic to overpower Rosalind, but the ring of courage gave her the bravery to face the sorceress' magic, and the ring of wisdom gave her the knowledge to defeat the sorceress.

Sorceress: "Give me the rings, young girl! I want their power for myself!"

Rosalind: "I will never give up the rings. They are not just pieces of jewelry, they are symbols of courage, wisdom, and love. And I will use them to defeat you and protect the kingdom!"

With the sorceress defeated, Rosalind became a hero in the kingdom. People celebrated her bravery and her use of the magic rings to defeat the evil sorceress and restore peace to the kingdom.

Rosalind decided to continue her journey, traveling from village to village and spreading the message of love and kindness wherever she went. She used the rings to help those in need and to bring hope to the hopeless.

One day, as Rosalind was on her way to help a village in need, she came across a young girl who was lost and afraid. The girl reminded Rosalind of herself when she first discovered the magic rings, and she knew that she had to help her.

Rosalind: "Hello there, young one. I'm Rosalind. What's your name?"

Young Girl: "My name is Elsie. I'm lost and I don't know how to get back home."

Rosalind: "Don't worry, Elsie. I'm here to help. And I have something special to give you."

Rosalind took off the rings and placed them on Elsie's fingers.

Rosalind: "These are the magic rings of courage, wisdom, and love. They will guide you on your journey and help you to be the best person you can be."

Elsie was overjoyed and thanked Rosalind for her kindness. And with that, Rosalind continued her journey, knowing that the magic of the rings would live on through Elsie and all the other young people she would help in the future.

The end.

The Boy Who Could Not Stop Jumping

Once upon a time, there was a young boy named Albert. Albert was an energetic and curious child who lived in a small village at the foot of a mountain. He had a unique talent that set him apart from all the other children in the village - he loved to jump. Albert would jump over rocks, jump from tree to tree, and even jump up and down on his bed. He simply couldn't stop jumping, no matter what he was doing.

One day, Albert heard about a magical land on the top of the mountain where he could jump as high as he wanted. The land was said to be filled with riches beyond his wildest dreams, and Albert knew he had to see it for himself. So, he set off on a journey to the top of the mountain.

As Albert began his climb, he met a wise old man who lived at the base of the mountain. The old man warned Albert that the journey to the top would be difficult and that he would encounter many obstacles along the way. But Albert was determined and refused to listen to the old man's warning.

"I must reach the top of the mountain and see this magical land for myself!" Albert exclaimed. "I will jump over every obstacle in my way!"

And so, Albert continued his journey, determined to reach the top of the mountain and fulfill his dream.

Albert encountered many obstacles along the way, but he was true to his word and used his jumping abilities to overcome them. He jumped over rivers, climbed up steep cliffs, and even outsmarted a cunning fox who tried to trick him. As he neared the top of the mountain, Albert came across a large chasm that seemed impossible to cross.

"This is it," Albert thought to himself. "This must be the final test before I reach the magical land."

Albert took a deep breath and prepared to jump, but just as he was about to take off, he heard a voice behind him.

"Wait!" the voice said. "You cannot jump this chasm. It is too wide."

Albert turned around and saw a small, but wise, bird perched on a nearby tree.

"How am I supposed to reach the other side?" Albert asked.

"You must use your mind, not just your legs," the bird replied.

Albert thought about what the bird had said and realized that the bird was right. He couldn't simply rely on his jumping abilities to get him to the other side of the chasm. He needed to use his mind as well.

So, Albert closed his eyes and imagined a bridge spanning the chasm. When he opened his eyes, he saw that a bridge had indeed appeared, leading him safely to the other side.

"I did it!" Albert exclaimed. "I used my mind to overcome the obstacle."

With newfound determination, Albert continued his journey, finally reaching the top of the mountain. He was met with a magnificent sight - a magical land filled with riches beyond his wildest dreams.

Albert stood at the entrance, realizing that he had not only accomplished his goal but had also learned an important lesson about the power of his mind.

As Albert explored the magical land, he found that it was not just a place of riches, but also a place of challenges and tests. He was greeted by a wise old wizard who told him that he must prove himself worthy to stay in the land and inherit its wealth.

"You have proven your bravery and determination to reach the top of the mountain," the wizard said. "But the true test of your worth is whether you can overcome the challenges that lay ahead."

Albert was determined to prove himself, so he set out on a series of trials and tests, using both his mind and his jumping abilities to overcome each one. He solved puzzles, defeated beasts, and navigated treacherous mazes, always relying on his courage and wit.

Finally, after weeks of trials, Albert was declared worthy by the wizard and was given the key to the treasure trove of the magical land.

"You have proven yourself to be a true hero," the wizard said. "You have shown that you are brave, determined, and clever. You have used your mind as well as your jumping abilities to overcome the challenges you have faced. You are truly deserving of the riches that this land has to offer."

Albert was overjoyed and thanked the wizard for his wisdom and guidance. He gathered as much treasure as he could carry and set off back down the mountain, eager to return home and share his wealth with his family and friends.

As he walked down the mountain, Albert looked back and saw the magical land fading into the distance. He smiled, knowing that he would always treasure the lessons he had learned and the memories he had made on his journey.

The end.

The Great Forest Council

Once upon a time, in a dense and lush forest, the king of the animals, a wise old stag, was getting old. He knew it was time for him to step down and choose a new king to rule the forest.

So he called a meeting of all the animals to decide who would be the next king. The animals all gathered in a clearing in the forest, eager to hear what the stag had to say.

Stag: "My friends, I have called you here today to discuss a very important matter. As you all know, I am getting old and it is time for me to step down as king of the forest. We must choose a new king to rule our home."

The animals all looked at each other, wondering who would be chosen as the next king. Some were nervous, while others were excited at the prospect of ruling the forest.

Just then, a strong and proud lion stepped forward.

Lion: "I should be the next king. I am the strongest and bravest animal in the forest. I will protect and care for all of you."

The other animals looked at the lion skeptically. They knew he was brave and strong, but they also knew he could be quick to anger and sometimes selfish.

A gentle and wise deer then stepped forward.

Deer: "I would like to nominate a different animal to be the next king. A wise and just animal, who will always put the needs of the forest and its creatures first."

The animals all murmured in agreement, wondering who the deer would nominate.

The animals continued to debate and discuss the merits of different animals for the role of king. Some were in favor of the lion, while others thought the deer's nominee would be a better choice.

Suddenly, a small but cunning fox stepped forward.

Fox: "I have a solution to our problem. Let's have a competition to determine who will be the next king."

The animals all looked at each other, considering the fox's proposal. It seemed like a fair and impartial way to determine the next king.

And so, the animals agreed to hold a competition to determine who would be the next king of the forest. The competition would be a series of tests, to see which animal had the strength, wisdom, and courage to rule the forest.

The competition was fierce and intense, with each animal determined to be the winner. The lion was strong and brave, but sometimes rash. The deer's nominee was wise and just, but not as strong as the lion.

As the competition reached its final event, the animals were on the edge of their seats, wondering who would come out on top. The last event was a test of bravery and courage, and the winner would be crowned the new king of the forest.

The lion and deer's nominee stepped forward, ready to face the final challenge. They both knew that the outcome of this event would determine who would rule the forest for many years to come.

The final event of the competition was a dangerous and difficult journey through the forest. The lion and deer's nominee had to navigate through the forest, avoiding traps and overcoming obstacles, to reach a hidden treasure at the end.

As the two animals set out on their journey, the other animals watched with bated breath. They knew that this would be the true test of the next king's bravery and courage.

After a long and grueling journey, the lion and deer's nominee finally reached the hidden treasure. But as they approached, they were shocked to find that the treasure was not gold or jewels, but instead a beautiful and peaceful meadow.

Lion: "This is not what I expected. I thought the treasure would be gold or jewels."

Deer's nominee: "The true treasure is not something we can hold in our paws or hooves. It is the peace and happiness of the forest and its creatures."

The lion looked at the deer's nominee, seeing the wisdom and compassion in his eyes. He knew then that the deer's nominee was the true ruler of the forest.

And so, the deer's nominee was crowned the new king of the forest. The lion stepped back, proud to have competed in the fair and just competition. And the animals all lived happily ever after, under the wise and just rule of their new king.

The end.

The Adventures of Little-Handed Lila

Lila was a young girl with a big heart, but small hands. Despite her small size, she had a big imagination and a love for adventure. However, her small hands often made her feel like she could not do the things she wanted to.

One day, while wandering through the forest, Lila stumbled upon a mysterious book. As she opened the book, she was transported to a magical world where anything was possible.

Lila: "Wow, this is incredible! I never thought I would get the chance to explore a world like this."

As she explored the magical world, Lila met new friends and discovered new abilities she never thought she had. But she also encountered challenges that seemed impossible for her to overcome with her small hands.

Lila: "I know I have small hands, but I'm not going to let that stop me from having the adventure of a lifetime."

As Lila continued her journey, she encountered more and more challenges. But with each challenge, she found a way to use her small hands to her advantage. She discovered that her small hands were actually incredibly nimble and could fit into tight spaces that others couldn't.

One day, Lila and her friends came across a group of fairies who were in trouble. The fairies had lost their magic and were in danger of losing their home to a powerful evil sorceress.

Lila: "I have to help the fairies! I may have small hands, but I know I can find a way to save their magic and their home."

With determination in her heart, Lila and her friends set out on a quest to save the fairies. They traveled to the sorceress's lair and found that the source of the fairies' magic was locked away in a chest that was guarded by a powerful dragon.

Lila: "This dragon may be big, but I won't let it stop me! My small hands are going to come in handy for this."

Using her nimble hands, Lila was able to sneak past the dragon and unlock the chest. She retrieved the fairies' magic and returned it to them, restoring their home and their happiness.

Lila: "I did it! I never thought my small hands would be able to save the day, but they did."

With the fairies' magic restored, Lila and her friends were celebrated as heroes. The fairies showered them with gifts and thanked them for their bravery.

Lila: "I couldn't have done it without my friends. We make a great team!"

Lila returned home with a newfound confidence and appreciation for her small hands. She realized that her hands may be small, but they were full of strength and determination. From that day on, Lila never let her size stop her from achieving her goals. She continued to go on many adventures, using her small hands to overcome obstacles and help those in need.

Lila: "I may have small hands, but they're big in spirit. And that's all that matters."

The end.

The Tiny Adventurer and the Village of Giants

Once upon a time, there was a young girl named Ava who lived in a small village at the foot of a mountain. Ava was known for her bravery and adventurous spirit, but she was also very small compared to the other villagers.

One day, Ava heard rumors of a village of giants at the top of the mountain. She was fascinated by the idea and decided to set out on a journey to find them.

Ava: "I want to see these giants for myself. I bet they're not as scary as everyone says they are."

As Ava made her way up the mountain, she encountered many obstacles and challenges. But she never gave up, using her determination and quick thinking to overcome them.

Finally, Ava arrived at the entrance of the giant village. She was greeted by a giant guard who was twice her size.

Guard: "Who are you and what brings you to our village?"

Ava: "I'm Ava, and I've come to see the giants. I've heard so much about them and I want to learn more."

The guard let her in and Ava was amazed by what she saw. The village was filled with giant houses, giant trees, and giant flowers. And the giants themselves were huge, towering over Ava like giants in a fairy tale. But to Ava's surprise, they were kind and friendly, and she quickly made friends with them.

As Ava explored the giant village, she discovered that something was wrong. The giants were worried about a mysterious creature that had been causing trouble in the village. It was destroying their crops and homes, and they didn't know what to do.

Ava: "What kind of creature is it? Can I help in any way?"

Giant Leader: "We don't know what it is, but it's very powerful. It's too dangerous for you to go near it, Ava."

But Ava was not one to back down from a challenge. She offered to help find the creature and stop it from causing any more harm.

Ava set out to find the creature, determined to save the giant village. As she searched, she encountered many dangers, but she never gave up. Finally, she came face to face with the creature. It was a giant monster, with sharp claws and a fierce roar.

Ava: "I won't let you harm the giant village any longer. I'll stop you, even if I have to do it alone."

The creature lunged at Ava, but she was quick and clever. Using her small size to her advantage, she was able to dodge its attacks and find its weak spot. With one final blow, Ava defeated the monster and saved the giant village.

The giants were overjoyed and grateful to Ava for her bravery. They threw a big celebration in her honor, and Ava was hailed as a hero.

After the excitement of defeating the monster and saving the village, Ava began to feel homesick. She missed her own family and wanted to return home. The giants understood her feelings and offered to help her find her way back.

Ava: "Thank you for everything. I had a wonderful adventure here, but I must return home now."

The giants gathered some supplies for Ava and showed her the way back to her village.

When Ava returned home, she was greeted with open arms by her family and friends. They were amazed by her bravery and the incredible adventure she had been on.

Ava: "I never thought that my small hands would be a strength, but I learned that anything is possible if you believe in yourself."

From that day on, Ava was known as the girl who could do anything. She continued to go on adventures and face new challenges, always with the confidence that she could overcome anything that came her way.

And the giants? They remained close friends with Ava and were always ready to lend a helping hand whenever she needed it. The magical village of giants and the girl with small hands lived happily ever after.

The end.

The Greedy Girl and the Magic Forest

Once upon a time, in a kingdom far, far away, there lived a girl named Lilian. Lilian was a very greedy girl and she loved money more than anything else in the world. She would often go to the market and haggle with the merchants to get the lowest price for everything she bought.

One day, Lilian heard about a magical forest that was said to grant wishes to those who entered it. She thought to herself, "If I can find this forest and make a wish, I'll become the richest person in the kingdom!" So she set out on a journey to find the magic forest.

After many days of traveling, Lilian finally stumbled upon the entrance to the magic forest. She was overjoyed and quickly ran inside. As she walked through the forest, she came across a beautiful clearing with a pond in the center.

Suddenly, a voice called out to her. "Lilian, why have you come to this forest?"

Lilian turned around to see a wise old owl perched on a tree branch. She replied, "I have come to make a wish and become the richest person in the kingdom."

The owl shook its head and said, "Lilian, true riches cannot be found in material possessions. They come from within, from being content and happy with what you have."

Lilian didn't understand what the owl meant. She replied, "I don't want to be content, I want to be rich!"

The owl sighed and said, "Very well, make your wish."

Lilian closed her eyes and wished with all her heart to be rich. Suddenly, the pond in the clearing started to glow and coins started to rain down from the sky. Lilian was ecstatic and started to collect all the coins.

However, as she was collecting the coins, she realized that the more she collected, the heavier they became. She tried to run out of the forest, but she was too weighed down by the coins. She couldn't move and was trapped in the magic forest forever.

Days went by, and Lilian was still trapped in the magic forest. She tried to use all the coins she had collected to buy her way out, but no one in the kingdom was interested in her wealth. She started to realize that her greed had trapped her in the forest and that she needed to change her ways.

One day, as she was sitting by the pond, the wise old owl appeared again. Lilian was grateful to see him and asked for his help.

Lilian: "Oh wise owl, please help me. I am trapped in this forest, and I don't know how to get out."

Wise Owl: "Lilian, you must understand that you cannot buy your way out of this forest. You must first change your ways and learn to be content with what you have."

Lilian: "I understand that now, but I don't know how to change. Can you help me?"

Wise Owl: "Yes, I can help you. You must first give away all the coins you have collected. Only then will the magic forest release you."

Lilian: "Give away all my coins? But that's all I have!"

Wise Owl: "Yes, you must give them away. Only then will you learn to be content with what you have."

Lilian thought about the wise owl's words and realized that she had to make a decision. She could either keep her coins and remain trapped in the forest forever or give them away and learn to be content.

Lilian: "I will give away my coins."

She took all the coins she had collected and threw them into the pond. Suddenly, the magic forest started to change. The trees grew taller, the flowers bloomed brighter, and the sky cleared.

Wise Owl: "Well done, Lilian. You have learned the true meaning of wealth and happiness."

Lilian: "I have, wise owl. I have learned that wealth and happiness come from being content with what you have, not from material possessions."

Wise Owl: "You have indeed learned a valuable lesson. Now, go back to the kingdom and share your wisdom with others."

Lilian walked out of the magic forest a changed person, ready to share her wisdom with the world.

.

As Lilian walked back to the kingdom, she was greeted with amazement and surprise by the people she had once haggled with in the market. They could see the change in her and were curious to know what had happened to her.

Lilian told them about her journey to the magic forest and the lesson she had learned about the true meaning of wealth and happiness. The people listened in awe and many of them were inspired by her story.

Over time, Lilian became known as the wisest person in the kingdom. People would come from far and wide to seek her advice, and she would always share her wisdom with them. She lived a happy and contented life, surrounded by love and friendship.

The kingdom also changed for the better. People started to value relationships and happiness over material possessions, and the kingdom became a place of peace and prosperity.

Wise Owl: "Lilian, you have truly become a legend in the kingdom. Your story will be remembered forever and will inspire others to follow your path."

Lilian: "Thank you, wise owl. I am grateful for the lesson you taught me and for the journey that led me to become the person I am today."

The end.

The Magic Well of Youth

Once upon a time, in a far-off kingdom, there was a young girl named Claire. Claire was kind and brave, but she was also very curious. One day, while exploring the forests near her home, she stumbled upon a magical well.

Claire was amazed by the well and its sparkling waters. She leaned over the edge to take a closer look, and that's when she heard a voice.

Voice: "Drink from me, and you shall be granted one wish."

Claire was a little scared at first, but her curiosity got the better of her, and she reached down to take a sip of the water. As soon as she did, she felt a strange power coursing through her body.

Claire: "Who are you?"

Voice: "I am the spirit of the well. And I have granted you a wish. What do you desire?"

Claire thought for a moment and then spoke.

Claire: "I want to be able to travel the world and help people. But I'm still young, and I don't think people will take me seriously."

Voice: "Your wish is granted. From this day forward, whenever you drink from the well, you will age one year for every sip you take."

Claire was shocked but also very excited. She took another sip from the well and felt herself growing older, wiser, and more capable. She thanked the spirit of the well and set off on her journey, eager to use her newfound powers to help others.

As Claire traveled the kingdom, she used her newfound age and wisdom to help those in need. She would drink from the well and become older, gaining the experience and knowledge necessary to solve problems and make a positive difference in people's lives.

Soon, word of her abilities spread throughout the kingdom, and people began to seek her out for help. Claire became known as the "Magic Well Girl", and she was loved and respected by all.

However, there were also those who were jealous of her powers and wanted to use the well for their own selfish purposes. A group of greedy merchants discovered the well and started drinking from it, becoming older and more powerful themselves. They saw Claire as a threat and decided to capture her and take control of the well.

Claire was captured by the merchants and brought before their leader, a cruel and greedy man named Gort. Gort demanded that

Claire reveal the secrets of the well and give him control over its power.

Claire refused, knowing that the well was meant to be used for good, not for evil.

Gort: "You will tell me what I want to know or suffer the consequences."

Claire: "I will never reveal the secrets of the well. And I will never let you use its power for your own selfish purposes."

Gort was furious and ordered his men to hold Claire captive until she gave in. But Claire was brave and refused to be intimidated. She knew that she had to protect the well and stop the merchants from using its power for evil.

Days passed, and Claire continued to refuse to reveal the secrets of the well. The merchants grew more and more frustrated, but they were unable to break her spirit.

Meanwhile, news of Claire's capture spread throughout the kingdom, and people began to rally to her cause. A group of brave knights rode to the merchants' stronghold, determined to rescue Claire and protect the well.

The knights stormed the stronghold and defeated the merchants, freeing Claire from their captivity. Together, they returned the well to its rightful place in the forest, where it could be used for good once again.

Claire was hailed as a hero by the people of the kingdom, and she continued to use her powers to help those in need. The well became known as the "Well of Youth", and people would come from far and wide to drink from its waters and be granted a single wish.

Claire lived the rest of her life as a wise and respected leader, using her powers for good and spreading joy and happiness throughout the kingdom. And the magic well remained a symbol of hope and courage, inspiring generations to come.

The end.

The Great Forest Race

Once upon a time, in a lush and beautiful forest, all the animals decided to have a great running match to determine who was the fastest in the forest.

The race would be a long and difficult one, with many twists and turns through the forest. But the prize for the winner would be a delicious feast of their favorite foods, prepared by the other animals.

All the animals gathered together to hear the rules of the race and sign up to compete. There was the cheetah, known for his lightning speed, the rabbit, who was nimble and quick, and the tortoise, who was slow but steady.

As the day of the race approached, the excitement among the animals grew. Each animal was determined to win the race and earn the title of the fastest animal in the forest.

The starting gun fired, and the race was on! The animals took off, running through the forest, with the cheetah taking an early lead. But the rabbit and the tortoise were close behind, determined to catch up and win the race.

The animals raced through the forest, dodging trees and leaping over streams. The cheetah was still in the lead, but the rabbit and the tortoise were close behind.

As they reached the halfway point of the race, the cheetah started to feel his energy flagging. He had been running at full speed for so long, and he was starting to get tired.

Cheetah: "I can't keep this up. I'm starting to get tired."

Just then, the rabbit overtook the cheetah, putting him in the lead. The tortoise was still trailing behind, but he was steadily making progress.

Rabbit: "Ha! I'm in the lead now! No one can catch me!"

The cheetah tried to pick up his pace, but his legs felt heavy, and his breathing was labored. He was starting to fall behind, and he knew that if he didn't do something soon, he would never win the race.

The animals raced towards the finish line, their hearts pounding and their legs straining. The rabbit was still in the lead, but the cheetah and the tortoise were close behind.

Just as the rabbit was about to cross the finish line, he tripped on a branch and stumbled. He looked up to see the cheetah and the tortoise neck-and-neck, both determined to win the race.

The animals crossed the finish line, exhausted but elated. They had given it their all, and they were proud of their effort. But as they looked up at the scoreboard, they were shocked to see that they had all finished the race in the same time!

The animals were stunned. They couldn't believe that they had all finished the race in the same time. They gathered around the scoreboard, trying to make sense of what had just happened.

Rabbit: "This can't be right. I was in the lead!"

Cheetah: "I was so close. I thought I had it."

Tortoise: "I may have been slow, but I never gave up."

Just then, an old wise owl who had been watching the race flew down to join them.

Owl: "My friends, you have all won the race. For you see, it was not about who was the fastest, but about the effort you put into the race and the determination you showed."

The animals realized that the owl was right. They had all given it their all and had shown great determination. And so, instead of crowning one animal as the winner, they all feasted together, celebrating their effort and determination.

From that day on, the animals of the forest held the Great Forest Race every year, and it became a celebration of effort and determination, rather than just speed. And they all lived happily ever after, knowing that they were all winners in their own way.

The end.

The Fruits' Journey to Market

Once upon a time, in a lush fruit orchard, a group of fruits were getting ready for their journey to the market. They had heard that the market was a place where people from far and wide came to buy fresh produce, and they were eager to see it for themselves.

Apple: "I can't wait to show everyone how delicious and crisp I am."

Pear: "And I can't wait to show off my unique shape and sweet taste."

Strawberry: "I just hope we get picked. I don't want to end up on the ground, getting squished."

Banana: "Don't worry, Strawberry. We'll all be picked. We just have to be patient."

The fruits set off on their journey, their excitement building with every step. As they walked, they met other fruits and vegetables who were also on their way to the market.

Tomato: "Good luck, my friends! I hope you sell for a good price!"

Carrot: "I just hope someone appreciates my sweet and crunchy taste."

The fruits continued their journey, chatting and laughing, until they finally arrived at the market. They were in awe of the sights and sounds around them, and they couldn't wait to see what would happen next.

As the day went on, the fruits were taken aback by how many people came to the market to buy produce. They were also amazed by how many different kinds of fruits and vegetables were for sale. They saw fruits they had never seen before, and they marveled at the variety of shapes, sizes, and colors.

Apple: "Look at all these different types of fruits. I never knew there were so many!"

Pear: "I've never seen a fruit shaped like that before!"

Strawberry: "And look at all the different colors. It's so beautiful!"

Banana: "I'm so glad we came to the market. This is an amazing experience."

However, as the day wore on, the fruits started to get worried. They saw that some of the fruits and vegetables were not getting picked, and they feared that they would be left behind.

Just as the fruits were starting to lose hope, a kind old woman approached them. She looked carefully at each of the fruits, and then she turned to the fruits and said:

Old Woman: "I have been searching for the perfect fruits for my special recipe. And I have found them! You all look perfect to me!"

The fruits were overjoyed. They had finally found a customer who appreciated their unique qualities, and they were going to be a part of something special. The woman carefully selected each of the fruits, and she paid a fair price for them. The fruits were ecstatic, and they felt like they had truly accomplished something great.

As the old woman was leaving the market with the fruits in her basket, the fruits started to feel a sense of sadness. They had grown so close during their adventure, and now they were going to be separated.

Apple: "I'm going to miss you all so much."

Pear: "Me too. It's been such an amazing journey."

Strawberry: "But we'll always have this memory to cherish."

Banana: "And we'll always be a part of something special, no matter where we end up."

When the old woman arrived home, she carefully prepared the fruits for her special recipe. She baked a delicious pie with the fruits, and she served it to her friends and family. Everyone was amazed at the flavor and texture of the pie, and they asked the old woman where she had found such perfect fruits.

Old Woman: "I found them at the market, and I knew they would be perfect for my special recipe."

Everyone was impressed by the old woman's taste and judgment, and they marveled at the delicious pie. The fruits felt proud to have been a part of such a special dish, and they felt grateful for the adventure they had experienced.

And so, the fruits went on to live happy lives, knowing that they had been a part of something special and that they would always be remembered for their contribution to the delicious pie.

The end.

Rover's Homecoming Adventure

Once upon a time, in a small village, there lived a dog named Rover. Rover was a happy and friendly dog who loved to play and explore. One day, while Rover was out on a walk, he suddenly got separated from his owner. He was lost and didn't know how to get back home.

Rover: "Oh no! I'm lost! How am I going to find my way back home?"

As Rover walked through the forest, he met many different animals. They all offered to help him find his way home, but none of them knew the way.

Rabbit: "I'm sorry Rover, I don't know the way to your home."

Deer: "I wish I could help, but I don't know where you live."

Owl: "I'll keep an eye out for you, but I can't help you find your way home."

Rover was starting to feel hopeless, but he refused to give up. He continued on his journey, determined to find his way back home.

Rover: "I'll keep searching until I find my way back to my owner. I won't give up."

As Rover continued his journey, he encountered many obstacles along the way. He had to cross a fast-flowing river, climb a steep mountain, and avoid danger from wild animals.

Rover: "This is so hard! I wish I had someone to help me."

Just when Rover was about to give up, he met a wise old fox. The fox offered to help Rover find his way home if he agreed to help him find something that he had lost.

Fox: "I'll help you find your way home, but first, you must help me find my lost treasure."

Rover agreed, and the two set off on a journey to find the treasure. They searched high and low and finally found the treasure hidden in a cave.

As Rover and the fox were about to leave the cave, they heard a loud growl. A giant bear appeared and threatened to take the treasure for himself.

Bear: "That treasure is mine! Hand it over!"

Rover and the fox stood their ground, determined to protect the treasure. They worked together to come up with a plan and finally defeated the bear.

Fox: "Good work, Rover! We did it!"

Rover: "Thanks to you, Fox! I couldn't have done it without you."

With the treasure in hand, Rover and the fox set off to find Rover's home.

As Rover and the fox continued their journey, they began to feel tired. They stopped for a rest and decided to split the treasure between them as a reward for their teamwork.

Fox: "Here you go, Rover. Half the treasure for you and half for me."

Rover: "Thank you, Fox. This is more than enough for me."

As they rested, they talked about their adventures and became good friends.

Finally, after many days of traveling, Rover and the fox arrived at Rover's home. Rover's owners were overjoyed to see him again, and the fox went on his way, satisfied with his new friend and the treasure they had found together.

Rover: "Thank you so much, Fox. I'll never forget you."

Fox: "Goodbye, Rover. You're always welcome in the forest."

And with that, Rover settled back into life with his owners, happy to be back home and proud of the adventure he had been on. From then on, whenever he saw the fox, he would always remember the time they spent together and the treasure they had found.

The end.

The Cloud Princess

Once upon a time, in a kingdom high up in the skies, there lived a lonely girl named Amara. Amara lived on a cloud all by herself, surrounded by the beautiful clouds and twinkling stars. However, she felt very lonely and wished to make friends.

One day, Amara decided to explore the neighboring clouds. She put on her silver cloak and took off on her adventure. She visited cloud after cloud, but no one was there to play with her. Disappointed, she was about to return home when she saw a large, white cloud in the distance.

Amara: "I wonder what's over there. I haven't seen that cloud before."

Excited, she flew towards the cloud and landed on its soft, white surface. To her surprise, she saw a small village filled with friendly creatures she had never seen before. They had wings, long tails, and sparkly fur. They were called Cloudies.

Amara: "Hello! My name is Amara. I'm a Cloud Princess."

Cloudie: "Welcome, Princess Amara! We're Cloudies. We've been waiting for you. We heard that a new Cloud Princess had arrived in the kingdom, and we wanted to meet you."

Amara was overjoyed to have finally found friends. She spent the day playing games, flying, and having fun with the Cloudies. From that day on, she visited the village every day and made many new friends.

Amara: "I'm so happy to have friends to play with. I will never be lonely again."

And so, the Cloud Princess lived happily ever after, surrounded by her new friends, the Cloudies.

One day, while Amara was playing with the Cloudies, she noticed that the sky was getting darker, and the winds were getting stronger. She realized that a storm was coming.

Amara: "Oh no! A storm is coming. We need to protect the village."

Cloudie: "Yes, Princess. We have a safe place for us to hide during the storm, but the village needs to be protected too."

Amara and the Cloudies worked together to protect the village. They used their magic to create a shield around the village and make sure that the buildings and houses were secure. The storm was getting stronger and stronger, but Amara and the Cloudies stood their ground, determined to protect their home.

Suddenly, they heard a loud noise and the shield around the village started to crack. Amara realized that there was a big, dark cloud in the center of the storm that was causing all the damage.

Amara: "That dark cloud is causing all the damage. We need to stop it."

Cloudie: "But how, Princess? It's too powerful for us."

Amara: "We need to use our combined magic. We can do it. I know we can."

The Cloudies and Amara joined hands and focused their magic on the dark cloud. They poured all their love and light into their magic, and the dark cloud started to dissipate. The storm started to calm down and the sky cleared up. The village was safe.

Amara: "We did it! We stopped the storm and saved the village."

The Cloudies cheered and hugged Amara, grateful for her leadership and bravery. Amara felt proud of herself and grateful for her friends. She realized that there was no limit to what they could do when they worked together.

After the storm was over, Amara and the Cloudies started to clean up the village. They repaired the damages caused by the storm and made sure that everything was back to normal. The

Cloudies were amazed by Amara's bravery and leadership during the storm, and they were even more grateful to have her as their friend.

Days turned into weeks and weeks turned into months. Amara continued to visit the village and play with the Cloudies. She was no longer lonely, and she felt like she had found a place where she belonged. The Cloudies felt the same way and they cherished their friendship with the Cloud Princess.

One day, Amara received a message from the king of the sky kingdom. He had heard about her bravery during the storm, and he wanted to meet her. Amara was nervous, but she was also excited to meet the king.

Amara: "I'm so nervous, but I'm also excited. I can't wait to meet the king."

Cloudie: "Don't worry, Princess. You'll do great. We're all here for you."

Amara traveled to the king's palace and met him. The king was impressed by Amara's bravery and leadership during the storm, and he offered her a position as the protector of the sky kingdom. Amara accepted the offer and became the protector of the sky kingdom. She continued to visit the village and play with the Cloudies, but she also had a new purpose in life.

From that day on, Amara was no longer just the Cloud Princess, but also the protector of the sky kingdom. She was loved and respected by all the creatures in the kingdom, and she lived happily ever after, surrounded by her friends and her new purpose.

The end.

The Knitting Princess

Once upon a time, there was a young girl named Jenna. She lived in a small village surrounded by rolling hills and vast fields of flowers. Jenna was different from other girls her age. While they played with dolls or ran around, she loved to knit. She found peace and happiness in creating warm and cozy blankets, scarves, and hats.

One day, while she was knitting in her room, a fairy appeared. The fairy was small, with delicate wings and a sparkling aura.

Fairy: "Hello, Jenna. I have been watching you and I have seen the kindness in your heart. You have a special talent for knitting, and I have come to offer you a gift."

Jenna: "A gift? For me? What is it?"

Fairy: "I would like to give you the gift of magic. From now on, every time you knit, your creations will have the power to bring joy and comfort to those who use them."

Jenna was overjoyed. She had always dreamed of using her knitting to make a difference in the world. She hugged the fairy, thanking her for the gift.

Jenna: "Thank you so much! I promise to use my gift for good and bring joy and comfort to others."

Fairy: "I have no doubt that you will, Jenna. You have a kind heart and a true talent for knitting. Go now, and spread joy wherever you go."

And with that, the fairy disappeared, leaving Jenna to her knitting. From that day on, Jenna's creations were filled with magic, bringing comfort and happiness to all who used them. And Jenna lived happily ever after, using her gift to bring joy to the world.

Jenna continued to knit and her creations became more and more popular. People from all over the kingdom started to come to her village to see her work and to buy her blankets, scarves, and hats. Jenna was happy to help people and to spread joy wherever she went.

One day, a terrible drought hit the kingdom. The crops were failing, and the people were suffering. Jenna knew that she had to do something to help. She started to knit blankets and hats for the people in the kingdom, but she soon realized that she needed more materials. She decided to travel to the far corners of the kingdom to find the finest wool and the softest silk to make her creations even more special.

Jenna set off on her journey and traveled for many days and nights. She arrived at a remote village where she met a kind and gentle shepherd who offered to help her. The shepherd told Jenna about a magical sheep that lived on a nearby mountain. The sheep was said to produce wool that was so soft and warm that it could heal even the most broken hearts.

Jenna: "A magical sheep? Can you take me there?"

Shepherd: "I can, but the journey is dangerous. The mountain is home to many dangerous creatures, and the sheep is guarded by a fierce dragon."

Jenna: "I have to try. The people in my kingdom are suffering and I want to help them. Can you take me there?"

The shepherd agreed, and together they set off on their journey to the mountain. Jenna was determined to find the magical sheep and bring its wool back to the kingdom to help the people.

Jenna and the shepherd reached the mountain and began their ascent. They encountered many obstacles and faced many dangers, but they finally reached the top. There, they found the magical sheep, guarded by the fierce dragon.

Dragon: "Who are you and why are you here?"

Jenna: "I am Jenna, and I have come to find the wool of the magical sheep. The people in my kingdom are suffering, and I want to help them. Please, may I have some of the wool?"

Dragon: "The wool is precious and can only be given to those who are worthy. Prove to me that you are worthy, and I will give you what you seek."

Jenna thought for a moment and then took out her knitting needles. She started to knit a scarf, using only the softest and finest wool from the magical sheep. As she knit, she closed her eyes and thought of the people in her kingdom. She thought of the joy and comfort that her scarf would bring them. When she finished, she held the scarf out to the dragon.

Dragon: "You are worthy. Take the wool and use it for good."

Jenna thanked the dragon and gathered as much of the wool as she could carry. She and the shepherd returned to the kingdom, and Jenna started to knit. She used the magical wool to create the warmest and softest blankets, scarves, and hats that the kingdom had ever seen. People from all over the kingdom came to see her work, and they were filled with joy and comfort. The drought was lifted, and the kingdom was restored to its former glory.

And Jenna lived happily ever after, using her gift of magic to bring joy and comfort to the world. Her creations were cherished by all, and her name became known throughout the kingdom as the "Knitting Princess."

The end.

The Worrying Sun

Once upon a time, in a faraway kingdom, there lived a big and shining sun named Sol. Sol was the source of light and warmth for all the creatures of the kingdom and was loved by everyone. However, Sol was not happy. It was always worried about something or the other, and the kingdom was gradually becoming gloomy.

One day, the moon, who was Sol's best friend, noticed Sol's worry and asked, "What's bothering you, Sol? You don't seem yourself lately."

Sol replied, "Oh, Moon, I'm worried about my kingdom. I fear that I won't be able to provide enough light and warmth to the creatures of the kingdom forever. What if I get weak and stop shining one day?"

The moon, being wise and understanding, said, "Sol, you have been shining for millions of years, and I'm sure you'll continue to do so for millions more. You are the heart of the kingdom, and your light and warmth bring joy to all who live here. Have faith in yourself and don't let your worries weigh you down."

Sol smiled, "You're right, Moon. I shouldn't worry so much. I should trust in my strength and the love of the creatures of the kingdom."

And from that day on, Sol stopped worrying and shone brighter and happier than ever before. The kingdom was filled with warmth and light, and all the creatures lived in peace and happiness.

One day, an evil sorcerer entered the kingdom with a plan to extinguish Sol's light forever. The sorcerer had the power to control the clouds and make them cover Sol, blocking its light and warmth. The creatures of the kingdom started to feel the chill, and darkness began to spread everywhere.

The moon noticed this and went to Sol to inform him. "Sol, I've seen the clouds covering you. I think an evil sorcerer is trying to put out your light," said the moon.

Sol was horrified, "I can't let that happen. I need to do something to stop him."

The moon replied, "We'll stop him together. We'll go to the sorcerer and face him."

Sol and the moon traveled to the sorcerer's castle, where they confronted him. The sorcerer laughed, "You fools, you can't stop me. I have the power to extinguish your light forever."

Sol, brave and determined, replied, "You may have the power to control the clouds, but you don't have the power to extinguish the love and warmth in the hearts of the creatures of the kingdom.

They believe in me and my strength, and that is something no one can take away."

The sorcerer, realizing that Sol was right, became afraid. He knew that he couldn't defeat the love and warmth in the hearts of the creatures. He disappeared into thin air, and the clouds that covered Sol started to clear up.

After the sorcerer was defeated, Sol and the moon returned to the kingdom to bask in the love and adoration of the creatures. They were hailed as heroes and were celebrated throughout the kingdom.

Sol and the moon continued to shine and provide light and warmth to the kingdom, and they never forgot the lesson they learned. They realized that their strength and light came not just from within themselves but also from the love and belief of the creatures of the kingdom.

Sol said to the moon, "Moon, we've learned that the power of love and belief can defeat even the strongest evil. We'll always be grateful to the creatures of the kingdom for their love and support."

The moon smiled, "Yes, Sol. And we'll always be here to shine our light and spread warmth to all who need it."

And so, Sol and the moon continued to shine, bringing joy and light to the kingdom, for generations to come.

The end.

The Bunny Girl

Once upon a time, there was a little bunny named Thumper. Thumper lived in a forest with his bunny family and friends. One day, Thumper went for a walk and stumbled upon a magical flower. Without knowing, Thumper touched the flower and was transformed into a girl. Thumper was so shocked and didn't know what to do.

Thumper: "What happened to me? I'm a girl now!"

Thumper went back to her bunny family, but they didn't recognize her. They thought she was a stranger and chased her away. Thumper was so sad and didn't know where to go. She wandered in the forest until she stumbled upon a fairy named Glitter.

Thumper: "Please help me! I was a bunny, but now I'm a girl."

Glitter: "Oh my! That's a magical flower you touched. It can turn any animal into a girl. Don't worry, Thumper. I'll help you."

Glitter took Thumper to a hidden castle where she met other animals who were also turned into girls by the magical flower. They all lived in the castle and were trained by Glitter to become princesses.

Thumper: "Wow! I never knew there were other animals like me."

Glitter: "Yes, Thumper. And now, it's time for you to learn how to become a real princess."

Thumper was so excited to learn and started her training. She learned how to walk, talk, and behave like a real princess. She made new friends and had so much fun in the castle.

Thumper: "I never thought being a bunny girl would be so much fun."

And so, Thumper lived a happy life in the castle, learning and becoming a real princess. She never forgot her past as a bunny, but she was grateful for the new life she had. The end.

Years went by and Thumper became a beautiful and graceful princess. One day, the kingdom was in danger as an evil witch named Morganthe threatened to destroy it. Morganthe was jealous of the beautiful and kind princesses in the kingdom and wanted to destroy their happiness.

Glitter: "Thumper, the kingdom is in danger. Morganthe is planning to destroy it. We need your help to stop her."

Thumper: "Of course, I'll do anything to protect my kingdom and my friends."

Thumper and the other princesses went on a dangerous journey to stop Morganthe. They fought bravely against her minions and finally reached her castle.

Morganthe: "Ha! I finally have you all in my grasp. I will destroy this kingdom and rule over it as the only beautiful and powerful witch."

Thumper: "We won't let you do that, Morganthe. We will stop you and protect our kingdom."

The final battle began and Thumper and the other princesses used their magic and bravery to defeat Morganthe. It was a tough battle, but in the end, they succeeded and saved the kingdom.

Morganthe: "No! How could you defeat me? I am the most powerful witch in the land!"

Thumper: "Because we have the power of love and friendship. That's the real magic that can defeat any evil."

The kingdom was saved and Thumper and the other princesses were hailed as heroes. They returned to the castle, where they lived happily ever after.

After the victory over Morganthe, the kingdom was at peace once again. Thumper and the other princesses celebrated their victory with a grand feast and a ball. They danced and laughed, enjoying their newfound happiness.

Thumper: "I can't believe we defeated Morganthe and saved the kingdom."

Glitter: "Yes, Thumper. You and the other princesses are truly heroes. I am so proud of you all."

During the celebration, Thumper realized that she had the power to change back into a bunny. She was torn between staying as a princess or going back to her original form.

Thumper: "Glitter, I have a dilemma. I have the power to change back into a bunny. I don't know what to do."

Glitter: "It's a tough decision, Thumper. But you have to think about what makes you the happiest."

Thumper thought about it and realized that she was happy being a bunny girl. She loved the new life she had as a princess, but she also missed her bunny family.

Thumper decided to split her time between being a bunny and a princess. She would visit her bunny family and spend time in the forest, but also return to the castle to live as a princess. This way, she could have the best of both worlds.

Thumper: "I have decided to be both a bunny and a princess. I can visit my bunny family and also live as a princess. It's the perfect solution."

And so, Thumper lived a happy life, splitting her time between the forest and the castle. She was loved by all and remembered as the brave bunny girl who saved the kingdom.

The end.

The Girl and the Mimicking Monster

Once upon a time, there was a brave and curious girl named Jane. She lived in a small village surrounded by dense forests and tall mountains. One day, she decided to explore the forest to find new and exciting creatures.

Jane: "Today is the day! I'm going to explore the forest and discover new creatures."

As she walked through the forest, she came across a strange creature. It was big and furry with long arms and legs. But what was most surprising was its ability to mimic any sound it heard.

Jane: "Who are you? What are you doing here?"

The monster replied by mimicking Jane's voice perfectly.

Monster: "Who are you? What are you doing here?"

Jane was shocked but also fascinated by the creature's ability. She decided to name it Mimic.

Jane: "Hi Mimic! I'm Jane. What are you doing in the forest?"

Mimic: "Hi Jane! I live in the forest. I love to mimic the sounds I hear."

Jane and Mimic became fast friends and spent many hours exploring the forest together. Jane learned that Mimic was a kind and gentle creature, despite its scary appearance.

Jane: "Mimic, you're not like any other creature I've ever met. You're so special and unique."

Mimic: "Thanks, Jane. You're special too. I'm so glad we're friends."

One day, as Jane and Mimic were exploring the forest, they heard a loud rumbling noise. They followed the noise and found a group of hunters, who were capturing all the creatures in the forest.

Jane: "Mimic, we have to do something! These hunters are capturing all the creatures in the forest."

Mimic: "Yes, Jane. We have to stop them. But how?"

Jane had an idea and told Mimic to mimic the voice of a fierce and dangerous monster.

Jane: "Mimic, pretend to be a fierce monster. Maybe that will scare the hunters away."

Mimic agreed and started to mimic the voice of a monster. The hunters were scared and started to run away.

Just as the hunters were leaving, they spotted Jane and Mimic. They realized that the monster's voice was just a mimic and started to come back to capture them.

Hunter: "Ha! It was just a mimic. We can catch them now."

Jane and Mimic were in trouble, but they didn't give up. They used all their courage and bravery to fight the hunters and protect the creatures in the forest.

Jane: "We won't let you harm the creatures in the forest! We'll fight you with all our might!"

Mimic: "Yes, we'll protect the creatures and the forest!"

The battle was intense, but Jane and Mimic were determined to protect their friends and home. They fought with all their strength and finally, the hunters were defeated.

After the battle, Jane and Mimic were exhausted but happy. They had saved the creatures in the forest and protected their home.

Jane: "Mimic, we did it! We saved the creatures and the forest."

Mimic: "Yes, we did it together. We're a great team."

The creatures in the forest thanked Jane and Mimic for their bravery and kindness. They decided to celebrate their victory and honor their new heroes.

Creature: "Jane and Mimic, you are our heroes. We'll never forget your bravery and kindness."

Jane and Mimic felt proud and grateful. They had made new friends and had an adventure they would never forget.

Jane: "Mimic, this has been the best adventure of my life. I'm so glad we're friends."

Mimic: "Me too, Jane. This is just the beginning of our adventures together."

And so, Jane and Mimic continued to explore the forest, make new friends, and have many more adventures. They lived happily ever after, surrounded by the creatures they loved and protected.

The end.

The Brave Girl Who Conquered Her Fear of Thunder

Once upon a time, in a small village, there lived a young girl named Lirien. She was kind, brave, and loved by all in the village. But, there was one thing that made her tremble with fear - the sound of thunder. Whenever she heard it, she would hide under her bed covers and shake with fear.

One day, Lirien decided she had enough of being afraid. She wanted to conquer her fear and be brave like her friends. So, she set out on a journey to find the source of thunder and face her fear head-on.

As she traveled through the forest, she met a wise old owl who had lived there for many years. The owl asked Lirien where she was going and she told him about her quest to conquer her fear of thunder. The owl smiled and said, "My dear child, the thunder you hear is just the voice of the sky, shouting its joys and sorrows."

Lirien was curious and asked the owl to show her the source of the thunder. The owl agreed and flew with Lirien to a high mountain. There, Lirien saw the source of the thunder for the first time. It was a magnificent sight to behold - lightning bolts flashing across the sky and thunder echoing through the mountains.

Despite her initial fear, Lirien stood bravely and watched the thunder and lightning in awe. As she stood there, she realized that there was nothing to be afraid of. The thunder was just a part of nature, and there was nothing harmful about it.

Lirien returned to the village a new person - fearless and brave. From that day on, whenever she heard thunder, she would stand outside and watch it in awe, smiling at its beauty.

The villagers were amazed at the change in Lirien and admired her bravery. And from that day on, Lirien was known as the Brave Girl Who Conquered Her Fear of Thunder.

Years went by and Lirien grew into a strong and confident young woman. One day, she received a message from the wise old owl she had met so many years ago. The message said that the village was in danger and that Lirien was the only one who could save it.

Lirien immediately set out on a journey to the village and arrived to find that a fierce storm had struck and caused a great deal of damage. The villagers were frightened and did not know what to do.

Lirien stepped forward and declared, "Do not fear, for I am here to help!"

The villagers were amazed at Lirien's bravery and listened closely as she explained her plan. She would brave the storm and find the source of the trouble, putting an end to it once and for all.

Lirien set out into the storm, facing the rain, wind, and lightning with determination. As she approached the source of the trouble, she came face to face with a giant thundercloud, bigger and more frightening than any she had ever seen before.

The thundercloud spoke in a booming voice, "Who dares to face me and my power?"

Lirien stepped forward bravely and replied, "I do. I am Lirien, the Brave Girl Who Conquered Her Fear of Thunder. I am not afraid of you or your power."

The thundercloud was taken aback by Lirien's bravery and asked, "Why are you not afraid? Don't you know that I have the power to destroy anything in my path?"

Lirien replied, "I may have been afraid of thunder once, but I have learned that it is just a voice of the sky, shouting its joys and sorrows. I am not afraid of you or your power, for I know that nature is to be respected, not feared."

The thundercloud was impressed by Lirien's words and asked, "What can I do to help you, brave girl?"

Lirien replied, "Please, stop the storm. The village and its people are in danger."

The thundercloud listened to Lirien's request and immediately began to calm the storm. The rain stopped, the wind died down, and the lightning disappeared.

Lirien returned to the village with the news that the storm was over and the villagers were overjoyed. They thanked Lirien for her bravery and praised her for being such a strong and courageous young woman.

The wise old owl appeared once again and said, "Lirien, you have shown the world that even the bravest of heroes can be made by facing and overcoming their fears. Your bravery and kindness will always be remembered and admired."

The end.

The Adventure of the Girl and the Turtle

Once upon a time, in a small village by the sea, there lived a young girl named Nalini. She was adventurous and loved to explore the world around her. One day, while she was playing on the beach, she came across a tiny turtle.

Nalini was fascinated by the turtle and asked, "Where are you going, little turtle?"

The turtle replied in a small voice, "I am on a journey to find the biggest and most beautiful ocean in the world. Will you come with me and help me on my quest?"

Nalini was thrilled by the idea of a new adventure and replied, "Of course! I would love to help you find the biggest and most beautiful ocean in the world."

Nalini and the turtle set out on their journey, traveling over hills, through forests, and across rivers. They met many creatures along the way, but none of them had seen the ocean that the turtle was searching for.

Finally, they came to a large mountain and the turtle said, "I have a feeling that the ocean we are searching for is on the other side of this mountain."

Nalini and the turtle began to climb the mountain, facing many challenges along the way. But their determination and bravery helped them to overcome each obstacle, and finally, they reached the top of the mountain.

From the top of the mountain, Nalini and the turtle could see a vast, blue expanse of water that stretched as far as the eye could see. The turtle said in wonder, "This must be it! This must be the biggest and most beautiful ocean in the world!"

Nalini and the turtle smiled at each other, their hearts filled with joy and excitement as they gazed out at the magnificent sight before them. And so, their adventure had only just begun.

Nalini and the turtle were about to start their descent down the mountain when they heard a loud, rumbling noise. They looked up and saw a group of humans approaching, carrying fishing nets and harpoons.

The turtle said in a panicked voice, "We must hide, Nalini. These humans are hunters and they will harm the creatures of the ocean."

Nalini was determined to protect the ocean and its inhabitants, so she bravely stepped forward and said, "Stop! You cannot harm the creatures of the ocean. They have as much right to live in this world as we do."

The hunters were taken aback by Nalini's bravery and they hesitated for a moment. But then their leader, a gruff man with a bushy beard, said, "Get out of our way, little girl. We have a job to do and we won't let some silly child stop us."

Nalini stood her ground and said firmly, "I won't let you harm these creatures. I'll fight for them if I have to."

The hunters laughed and started to close in on Nalini and the turtle, their weapons raised. The situation was tense and it seemed as though a battle was about to begin.

Just as the hunters were about to attack, a group of dolphins leaped out of the water and surrounded Nalini and the turtle. The dolphins communicated with Nalini and the turtle through clicks and chirps, telling them that they would protect them.

The hunters were intimidated by the dolphins and their bravery, and they slowly backed away, lowering their weapons. The leader of the hunters said, "We didn't know there was anyone living here. We won't harm the creatures of the ocean anymore."

Nalini and the turtle were overjoyed that they were able to protect the ocean and its creatures. They thanked the dolphins for their help and continued their journey, exploring the vast, beautiful ocean.

From that day on, Nalini and the turtle made it their mission to protect the ocean and its creatures, and they became known as the guardians of the sea. They spent the rest of their lives traveling the world, spreading their message of kindness and conservation.

The end.

The Story of the Dog with Big Feet

Once upon a time, in a village at the foot of a mountain, there lived a dog named Dan. Dan was a friendly and playful dog, but he was different from all the other dogs in the village. Dan had big feet!

Dan's big feet made it difficult for him to run and play with the other dogs. He often tripped and stumbled, causing the other dogs to laugh and tease him. Dan felt sad and alone, and he wished that he could be just like the other dogs.

One day, while Dan was out exploring the nearby forests, he came across a wise old dog who was sitting on stone. The old dog said, "Hello there, young dog. Why do you look so sad?"

Dan explained his situation to the old dog and said, "I have big feet and the other dogs make fun of me. I wish I could be just like them."

The old dog listened carefully and then said, "Big feet are not a bad thing, young dog. They are a special gift. With your big feet, you have the power to do great things."

Dan was skeptical at first, but he decided to trust the wise old dog. He set out on a journey to discover what he could do with his big feet.

Dan traveled over hills, through forests, and across rivers. He met many creatures along the way, each one offering their own advice and encouragement.

Finally, Dan came to a village that was being threatened by a powerful river that had overflowed its banks. The villagers were afraid and didn't know what to do.

Dan offered to help and used his big feet to create a dam that held back the river and protected the village. The villagers were amazed and grateful, and they cheered and celebrated Dan's bravery.

From that day on, Dan was no longer seen as the dog with big feet, but as the dog with big heart and a hero in the village. And he finally realized the true value of his big feet.

Dan continued on his journey, and before long, he came across a kingdom in peril. The kingdom was being terrorized by a giant dragon that was breathing fire and destroying everything in its path.

The villagers were afraid and had nowhere to turn. They had tried to defeat the dragon themselves, but it was too powerful for them.

Dan knew he had to help, and he bravely stepped forward to face the dragon. The dragon laughed when it saw Dan and said,

"What are you going to do, little dog? I am too powerful for you."

Dan stood tall and replied, "I may be small, but I have big feet and a big heart. I will not let you destroy this kingdom."

The dragon was taken aback by Dan's bravery and asked, "What can you possibly do to stop me?"

Dan replied, "I will use my big feet to create a trench that will redirect your fire away from the kingdom."

The dragon was impressed by Dan's bravery and cleverness and said, "Very well, little dog. I accept your challenge. Let's see what you can do."

Dan dug a deep trench with his big feet, directing the dragon's fire away from the kingdom and towards a nearby mountain. The dragon's fire roared through the trench, but Dan's plan worked, and the kingdom was safe.

The dragon was defeated, and the kingdom celebrated Dan's bravery with a grand feast in his honor. Dan was hailed as a hero, and his bravery was told in tales and songs for generations to come.

Dan eventually returned home to the village at the foot of the mountain, and he was no longer seen as the dog with big feet. He was now a respected hero and a true friend to all.

Dan continued to use his big feet for good, helping those in need and spreading joy and kindness wherever he went. He lived a long and happy life, always remembered as the dog who had a big heart and big feet.

And from that day on, Dan was never afraid of his big feet again, for he knew that they were his greatest gift and his greatest strength.

The end.

The Adventure of Rolling Stone

Once upon a time, in a far-off land, there was a small rolling stone named Rollo. Rollo was unlike any other stone in the land, for he had a heart full of wonder and a desire for adventure.

One day, Rollo was rolling down a hill when he heard a cry for help. He followed the sound and found a small bird who had fallen out of its nest and was stuck on the ground.

Rollo knew he had to help, so he offered to take the bird back to its nest. The bird gratefully accepted, and together, they began their journey.

As they traveled, Rollo and the bird encountered many obstacles and dangers. They had to cross a raging river, climb a steep mountain, and navigate through a dark forest.

Despite the challenges, Rollo never gave up. He used his rolling ability to help the bird over the obstacles, and he always kept a watchful eye out for danger.

Finally, they reached the bird's nest, high up in a tall tree. The bird was overjoyed to be back in its nest and thanked Rollo for his help.

As Rollo was about to say goodbye and continue on his journey, the bird offered to join him on his adventures. Rollo was delighted and happily accepted the bird's offer.

Together, Rollo and the bird set out on a new adventure, rolling and flying through the land, facing new challenges and making new friends along the way.

Rollo and the bird had been traveling for days and had come across a beautiful garden. They were admiring the sights and sounds when suddenly, they heard a loud noise coming from a nearby cave.

The noise was so loud that it echoed throughout the garden, frightening all the animals and causing the plants to shake. Rollo and the bird were curious, so they decided to investigate.

As they approached the cave, the noise grew louder and more intense. Rollo and the bird cautiously entered the cave and were met with a strange and wondrous sight.

There, in the center of the cave, was a giant crystal that was glowing with a bright light. The light was so bright that it filled the entire cave with a warm and inviting glow.

The bird asked, "What could this be, Rollo?"

Rollo replied, "I'm not sure, but I have a feeling that this crystal holds the key to our next adventure."

Rollo and the bird approached the crystal, and as they did, the noise stopped, and the crystal began to speak. The crystal told them of a magical land far away, where they could find new adventures and solve the mysteries of the world.

The crystal also gave them a map to guide them on their journey and warned them of the many dangers they would face along the way. Rollo and the bird were eager to embark on this new adventure, and they thanked the crystal for its guidance.

Resolution:

Rollo and the bird set out on their journey, following the map and facing new challenges and adventures along the way. They encountered many obstacles, but with their determination and courage, they were able to overcome them all.

Eventually, Rollo and the bird arrived at the magical land, and they were amazed by all the wonders they saw. They explored the land, solved its mysteries, and made many new friends.

And so, Rollo and the bird lived happily ever after, always seeking out new adventures and experiencing all the wonders the world had to offer.

The end.

Goblin with One Ear: An Unusual Adventure

Once upon a time, in a far-off kingdom, there lived a goblin named Gribble. Gribble was different from all the other goblins in the kingdom. He had only one ear, and because of this, the other goblins teased and bullied him. Gribble was tired of being different and decided to go on an adventure to find his true place in the world.

Gribble packed his bags and set out on his journey. He walked through the forest, climbed over mountains, and crossed rivers. One day, he came across a wise old owl who was sitting in a tree.

Gribble asked the owl, "Do you know of any place where I might belong?"

The owl replied, "You must follow your heart, Gribble. It will lead you to where you belong."

Gribble thanked the owl and continued on his journey. He walked for many days, and as he walked, he thought about what the owl had said. Gribble realized that he was searching for something more than just a place to belong. He was searching for adventure and excitement.

And so, Gribble continued on his journey, determined to find the adventure that he was searching for.

As Gribble continued his journey, he stumbled upon a beautiful, glittering crystal cave. The crystal walls glimmered and sparkled, and Gribble was in awe of its beauty. Suddenly, a voice echoed through the cave.

Voice: "Gribble, why have you come to this place?"

Gribble was surprised and answered, "I am searching for adventure and excitement, and I stumbled upon this beautiful cave."

Voice: "You have found what you seek, Gribble. You are the chosen one, and you have the power to bring peace to the kingdom."

Gribble was shocked and asked, "What do I need to do?"

Voice: "You must retrieve the Lost Diamond and return it to its rightful place. Only then can peace be restored to the kingdom."

Gribble was determined to complete this task, and he set off on a new adventure, to retrieve the Lost Diamond and restore peace to the kingdom.

Gribble traveled through treacherous forests and treacherous mountains, facing obstacles and challenges along the way. He encountered fierce beasts and treacherous terrain, but he never lost sight of his goal. With determination and courage, he finally found the Lost Diamond and retrieved it from its hiding place.

Gribble returned to the kingdom, where he was greeted as a hero. The Lost Diamond was returned to its rightful place, and peace was restored to the land. The other goblins no longer teased Gribble because of his one ear, but instead, they admired him for his bravery and determination.

Gribble realized that he didn't need to find a place where he belonged, as he belonged right where he was, among his own kind. The adventure had given him the confidence to be himself and embrace his differences. He lived the rest of his days as a hero, telling the story of his adventure to all who would listen.

And so, the kingdom was at peace, and Gribble was happy knowing that he had found not just a place to belong, but his true purpose in life.

The end.

The Dreamcatcher and the Girl

Once upon a time, there was a young girl named Luna who lived in a small village surrounded by forests and mountains. Luna was a curious girl and loved to explore the forests. One day, she came across an old woman who was sitting outside her cabin. The old woman was weaving a dream catcher.

Luna asked the old woman, "What are you making?"

Old woman: "I am making a dream catcher. It is said to catch good dreams and keep them with you forever."

Luna was fascinated by the dream catcher and asked if she could help. The old woman agreed, and Luna spent the next few days helping her weave the dream catcher. As they worked, the old woman told Luna about the power of dreams and how important it was to have good dreams.

Luna: "How can I make sure I have good dreams?"

Old woman: "You must believe in the power of your dreams and never give up on them. The dream catcher will help, but it is up to you to chase your dreams."

Luna was determined to follow her dreams, and she hung the dream catcher above her bed. Every night, she went to sleep with a smile on her face, knowing that the dream catcher would catch her good dreams.

As Luna slept, she began to have incredible dreams filled with adventure and excitement. She dreamed of exploring new lands, meeting new friends, and achieving her greatest desires. Each night, her dreams grew more vivid and exciting. Luna was filled with joy and excitement, knowing that she was on the path to achieving her dreams.

One night, Luna's dreams took a dark turn. She dreamed that she was lost in a dark forest, and no matter which way she turned, she couldn't find her way out. She was scared and alone, and she felt like she would never find her way back. Suddenly, she heard a voice calling to her.

"Luna, follow my voice. I can help you find your way back."

Luna followed the voice, and she soon came to a clearing in the forest. In the center of the clearing stood a tall, regal figure. It was the old woman from the village, and she was holding the dream catcher.

Old woman: "Luna, you must listen to me. Your dreams have taken a dark turn because you have lost faith in yourself. You must believe in the power of your dreams and never give up on them. The dream catcher will catch your good dreams, but it is up to you to chase them."

Luna realized that the old woman was right. She had let her fears and doubts get the best of her, and she had lost faith in herself. But she was determined to change that. She took a deep breath and looked up at the old woman.

Luna: "I believe in myself and in the power of my dreams. I will never give up on them."

With that, Luna took the dream catcher from the old woman and held it tightly. She closed her eyes and concentrated on her dreams. Slowly, her surroundings began to change, and she found herself back in her own bed. She smiled, knowing that she was back on the path to achieving her dreams.

Luna spent the next few weeks following her dreams and chasing them with all her heart. She learned to believe in herself and her abilities, and she was amazed at what she was capable of. The dream catcher continued to catch her good dreams, and she felt more confident and empowered every day.

Eventually, Luna's hard work paid off. She accomplished her dream of becoming a successful artist, and her paintings were displayed in galleries all over the world. People were drawn to her unique style and the magic that seemed to shine through in her work.

Years later, Luna was walking through the village and came across the old woman who had given her the dream catcher. The old woman smiled and greeted her warmly.

Old woman: "Luna, it is good to see you. You have come a long way since I last saw you."

Luna smiled and hugged the old woman.

Luna: "Thank you for everything. The dream catcher you gave me changed my life. I learned to believe in myself and my dreams, and I was able to achieve them. I will never forget your kindness."

The old woman smiled and patted Luna's hand.

Old woman: "You were always meant for great things, Luna. The dream catcher simply helped you to see it."

And with that, Luna went on her way, grateful for the magic of the dream catcher and the lessons it had taught her. She continued to chase her dreams and live her life to the fullest, and she was always reminded of the power of believing in oneself.

The end.

The Magic Mirror's Secret

Once upon a time, in a small village, there lived a young girl named Sindy. She was known for her kindness and her gentle heart, but she often felt unsure of herself. She often wondered what it would be like to be more confident and adventurous, like the brave knights she had read about in books.

One day, while exploring the woods, Sindy stumbled upon an old, dusty shop. The shopkeeper greeted her warmly and invited her inside.

Shopkeeper: "Welcome, young one! What brings you to my shop today?"

Sindy explained that she was just exploring the woods and stumbled upon the shop. The shopkeeper nodded and then gestured to a large, ornate mirror hanging on the wall.

Shopkeeper: "This is a magic mirror, my dear. It will show you the truth about who you really are."

Sindy was skeptical at first, but the shopkeeper convinced her to take a closer look. As she gazed into the mirror, she was shocked to see her reflection change. Suddenly, she saw herself as a brave and confident adventurer, just like the knights she had read about. She gasped in amazement.

Shopkeeper: "You see, my dear? This mirror shows you the truth about who you really are. You have a brave heart and a spirit that is ready for adventure. All you need to do is believe in yourself."

Sindy was amazed by what she saw in the mirror and she felt a sense of excitement growing within her. She knew that she had to find a way to bring out the adventurer within her, and the magic mirror seemed like the perfect place to start.

Sindy continued to gaze into the magic mirror, determined to unlock its secrets. Suddenly, she saw something in the reflection that made her heart race. It was a map! A map that showed the location of a hidden treasure.

Sindy: "Is this real? Is the treasure real?"

Shopkeeper: "Yes, my dear. The treasure is real, but finding it will not be easy. The journey will test your bravery and your wit."

Sindy was determined to find the treasure and prove to herself that she was truly brave and adventurous. She thanked the shopkeeper and set off on her journey, following the map she had seen in the magic mirror.

As she journeyed deeper into the wilderness, Sindy encountered obstacles and challenges. But she didn't give up, she remembered what she had seen in the mirror and believed in herself. She was ready for the adventure of a lifetime.

After many days of travel, Sindy finally reached the location indicated on the map. She could hardly contain her excitement as she approached the spot, her heart pounding with anticipation.

Sindy: "This must be it! The place where the treasure is hidden!"

As she looked around, Sindy saw a large rock that seemed to be out of place. She approached it, and to her surprise, the rock began to glow. She realized that it was the key to unlocking the treasure. She pushed the rock with all her might, and a hidden door slowly creaked open.

Sindy stepped into the secret chamber and was stunned by what she saw. The room was filled with glittering gems, sparkling gold coins, and precious treasures beyond her wildest dreams. She had found the treasure, and her journey had been a complete success.

Sindy: "This is amazing! I did it! I found the treasure!"

Sindy gathered as much treasure as she could carry and made her way back to the shopkeeper. She thanked him for his guidance and gave him a share of the treasure as a token of her gratitude.

From that day on, Sindy was known as the bravest and most adventurous girl in all the land. She lived a life filled with joy, laughter, and adventure, and she never forgot the magic of the mirror that had started it all.

The end.

The Squirrel's New Wings

Once upon a time, there was a tiny squirrel named Skippit who lived in the forest with his family. Skippit was known for his curious and adventurous spirit, always exploring the forest and playing with his friends.

One day, Skippit came across a mysterious fairy named Twinkles who lived in a hidden glade deep in the forest. Skippit was amazed by Twinkles and asked her for a wish. Twinkles smiled and granted Skippit's wish to have the ability to fly.

The next morning, Skippit woke up with a pair of beautiful wings on his back. Excited to try out his new ability, Skippit flapped his wings and flew up into the sky. However, as he was soaring through the air, he suddenly realized that he was no longer a squirrel. Instead, he had transformed into a pigeon.

Skippit was shocked and confused. He flew down to the ground to talk to Twinkles, who explained that the wish had a catch. Skippit could fly, but he would be a pigeon forever. Skippit was saddened by the news but decided to make the most of his new form.

"Don't worry, Skippit," said Twinkles. "You may look different now, but your adventurous spirit will always be the same."

Skippit took to the skies, discovering new places and making new friends as a pigeon. Though he missed his squirrel life, he learned to love his new wings and the freedom they brought him.

One day, Skippit flew into a village where he overheard a group of birds talking about a great danger. A terrible storm was heading towards the forest and it was said to be the worst storm in years.

Skippit was worried about his family and friends who lived in the forest. He flew back to the forest to warn them, but they didn't believe him. They thought that Skippit was just telling tales to get attention.

"Skippit, why should we believe you? You're just a silly pigeon now," said one of his old squirrel friends.

Skippit was hurt by his friend's words, but he didn't give up. He decided to gather proof of the storm and show it to his friends and family. He flew back to the village and gathered some of the birds to help him.

Together, they flew to the edge of the storm and saw how massive and dangerous it was. Skippit and the birds flew back to the forest and showed the evidence to the other animals.

"We need to find shelter before the storm hits," said Skippit. "Let's work together to find a safe place for all of us."

The animals listened to Skippit and started working together to find shelter. They built sturdy shelters and gathered food and supplies to last them through the storm.

"Thank you, Skippit," said his old friend. "I'm sorry I didn't believe you earlier. You're not just a silly pigeon anymore, you're a true leader."

The storm hit the forest with full force, but Skippit and the animals were safely sheltered. They huddled together and listened to the raging winds and rain outside. Skippit was proud of the work they had done and grateful for the support of his friends and family.

After the storm had passed, Skippit and the animals ventured outside to assess the damage. They were relieved to see that the shelters had protected them, but the forest was in shambles. Trees were down, and the river was flooded.

"What do we do now?" asked one of the animals.

Skippit looked around and saw that the other animals were looking to him for guidance. He remembered the words of Twinkles and his own adventurous spirit.

"We rebuild," said Skippit. "We help each other and make the forest beautiful again."

And so, the animals worked together to clean up the forest and rebuild their homes. Skippit was happy to see how well everyone worked together, and he was proud to be a part of it.

Years passed, and the forest was once again a beautiful and thriving place. Skippit continued to fly and explore, but he always remembered the storm and the lesson it taught him. He learned that working together and supporting one another was the key to happiness and success.

The end.

The Girl with a Thousand Hats

Once upon a time, there was a young girl named Millie who lived in a small village. Millie was known for her love of hats. She loved trying on different hats and finding the perfect one to match her outfit.

One day, Millie heard about a Night for Girls, a special event where all the girls in the village got together to dance and have fun. Millie was so excited to attend the event and show off her latest hat collection.

When she arrived at the Night for Girls, she saw that all the other girls were wearing simple headbands or ribbons in their hair. Millie felt self-conscious about her elaborate hats and started to feel out of place.

"What's wrong, Millie?" asked one of her friends. "You always look so happy in your hats."

"I just feel like I don't belong here," said Millie, looking down at her hat. "Everyone else is wearing simple headbands, and I'm wearing a big, fancy hat."

Her friend smiled and took her hand. "Millie, you should never be afraid to be yourself. You love hats, and that's what makes you unique and special. Why don't you show everyone your collection?"

Millie smiled and nodded. She took a deep breath and walked to the center of the room, where all the girls were gathered.

"Hello, everyone!" said Millie, with a smile. "I love hats, and I wanted to show you my collection. I hope you like them!"

And with that, Millie began to twirl and dance, showing off her hat collection to the other girls. They gasped in amazement at the beautiful and colorful hats, and soon everyone was trying on the hats and having a great time.

Millie was so happy that she had been brave enough to be herself, and she learned that it was okay to stand out from the crowd. From that day on, she wore her hats with pride and never felt self-conscious again.

As the Night for Girls was winding down, Millie noticed a group of girls huddled together, whispering and looking at her. She felt a knot form in her stomach, thinking they were laughing at her hats.

Just as she was about to leave the event, the group of girls approached her. "Millie, we have a problem," said one of the girls. "Our headbands and ribbons have all broken, and we don't have anything to wear in our hair for the big parade tomorrow."

Millie looked at the girls, their faces filled with concern, and she knew what she had to do. "Don't worry," she said. "I have an idea."

Millie gathered all of her hats and brought them to the girls. "You can each wear one of my hats for the parade tomorrow," she said.

The girls gasped in surprise and delight, and they hugged Millie, thanking her for her kindness. Millie was happy to share her love of hats with the other girls and was excited to see them all in her collection during the parade the next day.

The next day, the girls gathered for the parade, all wearing one of Millie's hats. The crowd was amazed at the beautiful hats and the girls received many compliments. Millie felt proud and happy to share her passion with others.

After the parade, the girls returned the hats to Millie, and she was overwhelmed with gratitude. She realized that sharing her love of hats with others had brought her joy and happiness.

From that day on, Millie continued to collect hats and would often share them with others. She became known as the Hat Lady in the village and was loved and respected by all.

Millie never forgot the lesson she learned at the Night for Girls: that it was okay to be different and to stand out from the crowd.

She embraced her love of hats and encouraged others to be themselves, no matter what others might think.

And Millie lived happily ever after, surrounded by a community of friends who appreciated her for who she was and her love of hats.

The end,

The Boy and His Shells

Once upon a time, there was a young boy named Felix who lived by the sea. Felix loved to spend his days collecting shells on the beach. He would search for hours, picking out the most beautiful and unique shells he could find.

Felix had a special room in his house where he kept all of his shells, and he would often spend hours admiring them and organizing them into different collections. He was especially proud of his rarest shells, and he would often show them off to anyone who would visit his room.

One day, Felix's mother came to him with a worried look on her face. "Felix, I'm afraid we have to move away from the sea," she said. "Your father has found a new job in the city, and we have to leave in a week."

Felix was heartbroken. He loved his shells, and he didn't want to leave them behind. He asked his mother if he could bring his shells with him, but she told him that they wouldn't fit in the carriage, and they wouldn't have room for them in their new home.

Felix felt sad and lost. He didn't know how he was going to leave his beloved shells behind. He lay on his bed, staring at his collection and wondering what to do.

Felix's sadness turned to determination as he had an idea. He gathered all his shells and took them to the beach. He began to build a sandcastle, bigger and grander than any he had ever built before. He worked tirelessly, using all his shells to decorate the castle.

Soon, word of Felix's magnificent sandcastle spread through the village, and people from all over came to see it. They were amazed at the beauty and creativity of the castle, and many commented on how much Felix's shells added to the overall design.

Felix beamed with pride as he stood next to his creation. He realized that he didn't have to leave his love of shells behind - he could take it with him wherever he went. And even though he was moving away from the sea, he could still find joy in his love of shells and in creating beautiful things.

As Felix packed up his belongings to move to the city, he took special care to pack his shells. He knew they were valuable to him, but he also realized they had value to others as well.

When Felix arrived at his new home in the city, he immediately set to work decorating his room with his shells. He created a beautiful display and invited his friends over to see it. They were amazed at his collection and his creativity, and they quickly became his biggest fans.

Felix's love of shells continued to bring him joy, and he would often share his collection with others. He became known in the city as the Shell Boy and was loved and respected by all who knew him.

Felix never forgot the lesson he learned at the beach: that it was okay to be different and to embrace his passions, no matter where life took him. And he lived happily ever after, surrounded by his love of shells and the friends he made because of it.

The end.

Printed in Great Britain
by Amazon

19077555R00120